THE BEAT

"May we come in?" the suit said, almost pushing her aside as he entered the hall. The other one followed, and shut the door behind him.

"I … er…" The first chilly flicker of suspicion crossed Joanne's mind.

Suit smiled benignly. "Sit down, would you, Mrs Evans? It'll make things easier."

"What things?" Joanne found herself sitting down in the chair by the phone. "Where's your warrant card?"

The suit reached into the inside of his jacket and produced a revolver.

"This is my warrant card," he said, as Leather Jacket put a hand over Joanne's mouth. "Stay calm, please. Nobody will get hurt as long as you do exactly what I say."

Visit David Belbin's homepage at
http://www.geocities.com/SoHo/Lofts/5155

POINT CRIME

THE BEAT

Night Shift

David Belbin

SCHOLASTIC

Scholastic Children's Books
Commonwealth House, 1–19 New Oxford Street,
London WC1A 1NU, UK
a division of Scholastic Ltd
London ~ New York ~ Toronto ~ Sydney ~ Auckland

First published in the UK by Scholastic Ltd, 1998

Copyright © David Belbin, 1998

ISBN 0 590 19397 X

Typeset by TW Typesetting, Midsomer Norton, Somerset

Printed by Cox & Wyman Ltd, Reading, Berks.

10 9 8 7 6 5 4 3 2 1

For Stanley and Margaret

The city in these pages is real. The events described in them are not. All of the characters, together with the police station where some of them work, are imaginary. The author wishes to thank the many people, including serving police officers, who helped him with this series. He alone is responsible for any mistakes.

PROLOGUE

It was three in the afternoon when the doorbell rang. No one visited Joanne at this time of day unless they were selling something. That, or the Jehovah's Witnesses, which amounted to the same thing. Joanne didn't hurry to answer it. When Arthur, her husband, retired from the prison in three month's time, he could be the one who dealt with unexpected callers.

Joanne rehearsed what she'd say as she opened the door, not giving them a chance to speak. "I'm sorry. I never buy anything on the doorstep," was one response she used. The other was: "No thanks, we're all heathens here." Really, she and Arthur were Quakers.

The doorbell rang again, more insistently this time. Joanne was nearly at the door, but decided to ignore it. She could do without the aggro. Probably some spotty youth with a hard luck story, flogging over-priced cleaning materials. But then she had her doubts. Suppose, just suppose, it was someone else, someone she knew? Joanne took a look through the fish-eye security hole and saw a man in a suit.

"Who is it?" she called reluctantly.

"Police," a smart-sounding voice returned. "It's nothing to worry about, Mrs Evans, but if we could have two minutes of your time…"

They knew her name, so that was all right. The man was holding out his wallet. Joanne could see his warrant card. Not that she had time to make out his name. By the time she'd opened the door, he'd put it away again. He wasn't alone. The other one was balding and wore a leather jacket.

"May we come in?" the suit said, almost pushing her aside as he entered the hall. The other one followed, and shut the door behind him.

"I … er…" The first chilly flicker of suspicion crossed Joanne's mind.

"Your husband's at work, isn't he?" Leather Jacket said.

"Yes. He doesn't get home until just after ten."

"Good. That's what we wanted to hear."

"What is this?" Joanne asked. "Show me your identification properly, please."

Suit smiled benignly. "Sit down, would you, Mrs Evans? It'll make things easier."

"What things?" Joanne found herself sitting down in the chair by the phone. "Where's your warrant card?"

The suit reached into the inside of his jacket and produced a revolver.

"This is my warrant card," he said, as Leather Jacket put a hand over Joanne's mouth. "Stay calm, please. Nobody will get hurt as long as you do exactly what I say."

Prison works. That's what the politicians say. It's what they think the public wants to hear. *Yeah, right*, Joe thought. This was his first stint in an adult prison. In two weeks he'd learnt more about crimes and how to commit them than in three months at Glen Parva, the youth detention centre. When Joe got out, he wasn't going to go straight – who'd give him a job with his record? No, he was going to go into the most profitable scams going and get other people to do the risky stuff. He'd make prison work for him.

He was in the old lifers' wing, on *Ones*, which meant the ground floor. It was just like the movies. Small cells with a crapper in the corner. Tiny windows with bars on the outside. You could just force through a bit of bread or fruit peel to bombard anyone foolish enough to walk by within ten metres of the building. There were four floors, with a steel safety net above the first and third, to prevent anyone from jumping to their death. It was like living in a cage. The place smelt of old cabbage and there were always keys jangling, doors slamming, people playing boom boxes. You couldn't think. At least the lifers used to get a cell to themselves. Joe had to share.

But Nottingham Prison was better than Glen Parva. It was cleaner and there was less bullying. The sweet smell of dope smoke drifted out of cells in the early evening, making the atmosphere more relaxed. Joe couldn't afford to buy any gear for himself, and didn't know anybody who'd sneak him some in on a visit. On remand, you could have as many visitors as you wanted, but no one came to see Joe. He was thinking of applying to work. You didn't have to, on remand, but it would pass the time, and he could do with the money. Now and then Joe's cell-mate, Griff, would split a smoke with him, going on all the time about what a wonderful life he had on the outside.

Like Joe, Griff was on remand, waiting to be tried for crack dealing. He was twenty-two, and drove a BMW on the out, *if* you believed his tales (most people gilded the lily in here). Joe was only eighteen. He should have been in Lincoln Prison, where they kept the prisoners on remand, but the police had put him in Nottingham because they wanted to keep questioning him. They needed him close at hand.

One of their own had been murdered – an inspector called Paul Grace. Both the local CID and some guys from a special task force were over every other day, offering Joe deals. They wanted him to identify the two members of the motorway team he'd seen with their masks off, the Saturday before last, when he bumped into them on a burglary. Joe claimed he hadn't seen their faces. The police knew he was lying, but so what? They couldn't prove it. And Joe was dead if he ever told, just like that police inspector who'd been shot outside his house ten days ago. You didn't mess with the motorway team, who were responsible for a series of big burglaries and kidnappings. They were *serious* criminals. If any of them ever did get put away, they'd be top dogs on the inside.

Griff liked to exercise. He had a big deal ready to go down when he got out, and wanted to be in shape. Joe didn't bother. He'd been threatened in the gym once, told in no uncertain terms what would happen if he was thinking of testifying against the motorway team. He thought he'd convinced the guy that there was no way he'd grass. All the same, he'd stayed away from the gym since. After all, the police kept coming to see him. If the motorway team got jittery, they might have Joe killed as extra insurance. So the only places where Joe hung out were the TV room and, this one, the library. He and Griff had the place to themselves, because Griff had insisted on coming the minute they'd finished their lunch.

Joe never borrowed anything. If they had some of those graphic novels, he might have taken one, but they didn't. Mainly, though, he came to the library for the quiet, to think. Which was worse, he wondered – years on the inside worrying about when somebody was going to stick a sharpened spoon in your back? Or being a grass on the outside, always on the move, scared witless every time there was a strange knock on the door?

Someone came into the library. Joe couldn't see who it was from where he was standing, but Griff could. He motioned Joe to keep quiet, then hissed at the new arrival.

"Over here!"

Footsteps. The next words Griff said were, "Are we on?"

Joe didn't hear a reply. He couldn't tell who Griff was talking to on the other side of the library shelves. But then he saw the fat bloke walking away. It was Gordon Loscoe, the one they said was a Lottery millionaire.

"Didn't know you knew him," Joe commented, as they walked past the librarian. Griff glared at him and Joe didn't speak again until they were on their own.

"What's up?" he asked. Had he broken some kind of code? The prison was full of unwritten rules – not the ones the screws gave out, but the ones the other inmates made up themselves. It was easy to put a foot wrong.

"Just keep your nose out," Griff said. "See nothing, hear nothing. Understand?" Joe shrugged. There was a white-haired prison officer standing at the end of the corridor.

"You two, come with me," the guard said. "Governor wants a word."

What would the governor want with him? Joe wondered. The guard looked pale, ill. Maybe it was a mistake. Griff still had that glare on his face, so Joe said nothing. Gordon Loscoe was waiting around the corner. The three of them followed the guard out of the block, going right past the governor's office, towards the sports field.

"Here's the key," the old guard said, handing it to Griff. "You're to make a run for the hut during supper. Lock yourself inside in case anyone checks it."

"And we won't be missed?" Griff asked.

"I'll make sure of that." The guard sounded frightened. He was sweating heavily.

"When will we be picked up?"

"I don't know anything else. Now, get in there, out of sight."

The three of them ducked into a disused Nissan hut.

"What's going on?" Joe asked, as soon as they were alone.

"Keep your voice down," Griff hissed.

"I thought it was just the two of us," Gordon whispered.

"Seems someone forgot to tell the guard," Griff commented, "or he was too scared to listen properly when his wife gave him the instructions. Point is, Joe, you got lucky. Two of us paid top whack, but you're coming along for a free ride."

"You mean…?" Joe couldn't believe his ears.

"That's right. We're escaping."

1

"Crime pays," Eddie Broom told Shirley Wilder, as the two of them sipped champagne in the South of France. It was an October night, with the sun nearly all gone, but the breeze still warm enough to beat the best of English summers. Not that either of them expected to see England again.

"Go on, then," Shirley said, as Eddie offered to top up her glass. "You've convinced me."

His digital phone rang. It was their one connection with home. Shirley hadn't been allowed to give her children the number, which she resented. She listened to one side of the conversation.

"Tonight?" Eddie said. "Fine. You'll tell Loscoe the arrangements we agreed? And the boy? What about the other one? Good. Are all three of you going? And after? Separate cars, I hope. All right. That'll do. Give me a call tomorrow then. Let me know that you made it to France. Excellent. Good luck."

He switched the phone off and turned to Shirley. "All set."

"Good," she said. "Will we see him?"

"I'll have to. You won't. I'm still not sure about helping that old soak Loscoe out. We nearly got caught because of him."

"Gordon's family. His Natalie's going out with my Curt."

Eddie frowned. "I reckon you pay a lot more attention to family than Gordon Loscoe does."

"I doubt that," Shirley said, and Eddie shut up. He knew that she felt guilty about leaving her kids behind. Curt was fifteen and still at school. She'd been a lousy mother to him, but that was better than no mother at all.

At least Curt had Julie to look after him. Shirley's daughter was seventeen, and had a nine-month-old daughter of her own. Shirley didn't like leaving her either, but this was a once-in-a-lifetime chance. Eddie was retiring, in a hurry. The choice he'd given Shirley was *pack your bags and come now or never see me again.* Not much of a choice when you're crazy about a bloke and he's just told you that he's got enough money stashed away to keep the both of you in luxury for the rest of your natural.

Eddie was a criminal – not a bad kind of criminal, compared to some she'd met. He did the planning work for big burglaries, the watching to see who went where and when, the organization of escape routes. He never did the actual burglaries, never had to hit anybody on the head. But he still took a twenty-five per cent share of the proceeds.

Stop feeling guilty! Shirley told herself. Sooner or later, everybody has to fend for themselves. Shirley's kids were learning the lesson earlier than most, that was all. She'd had this one chance of happiness in her rotten life, and she was taking it.

"Fancy a swim before dinner, duck?" Eddie asked.

"Why not?"

Eddie climbed on to the board and dived in at the deep end. Shirley took off her robe and climbed into the pool more cautiously, wading into the warm water until she was up to her neck in it.

"Welcome back," Jan Hunt, the shift sergeant, told Clare Coppola as she walked into the parade room. "We've missed you."

Clare half nodded, looking distracted. It must be horrible for her, Jan thought, coming back to the place where her boyfriend used to be the boss. Jan wouldn't have blamed Clare if she never put on a uniform again.

Clare had been to Paul Grace's funeral the day before. Her black hair was cut shorter than normal.

The style made her face look big and emphasized the grey lines beneath her eyes. It was only a few weeks since Clare's twenty-first birthday, yet, in the brash fluorescent light, she looked Jan's age, which was thirty.

Clare sat down next to Gary Monk, who lived in the same house as her. Already in the parade room was Ben Shipman, Gary's partner and mentor. Across the table from him was veteran copper John Farraday.

"We're getting a new recruit later," Jan said. "The boss is briefing her now." Neither Ben nor John knew who the new recruit was, but neither of them asked about it. Clare's return had put a choker on casual conversation. Clare and Gary already knew what was going on, but said nothing.

Jan continued her briefing. "Tim's off," she told John as she finished. "I want you to partner the new girl. Clare, come with me."

"Fine."

"There are three cars available, but…"

"I've got paperwork that needs to be ready for court tomorrow," Ben said.

"OK. You and Gary hold the fort. The rest of us will go out."

Two cars patrolling the area was par for the course. Most nights, there wasn't enough to keep both busy and one of them would be parked up at the station by 2 a.m.

Jan had already checked with CID: there were no new leads in the Paul Grace murder case. Every copper in the city had put in overtime to help track the killer down, but no witnesses had been found. No one had snitched on who the gunman was. So forget *new* leads – there were no leads whatsoever. The stupid thing was, everybody knew who was behind the killings: the motorway team. But three of them were behind bars at the time, put there by Grace himself. And the fourth, Eddie Broom, had been hundreds of miles away, in Glasgow. Neil Foster, Jan's friend and former colleague, thought that the team had a mole in the police force, which was why they avoided capture and how they knew when and where to find Paul Grace. Jan wasn't so sure.

Paul Grace's replacement, Tony Winter, came out of his office. "Time you lot were moving," he said.

Winter was a smallish man, two or three inches smaller than Jan, who was five ten. He had neat, jet black hair which he brushed over a small bald spot. Passed over for promotion in Mansfield CID, where he'd been a sergeant for some years, he'd moved back to uniform to become an Inspector. He was, at a guess, thirty-six.

"But before you go," the Inspector said, as Clare and Jan made for the door, "I'd like to welcome our returning probationer."

He emphasized that word *probationer*. Clare might have plenty of experience, but she'd only been in the force for a year and a bit. "And I wa t to introduce you to our newest recruit, also a p obationer, who's transferred over from South…"

Both Jan and Clare turne   look at Ben, who didn't know what was co

"I believe that most of   know Ruth already," the Inspector said, as   s ex-girlfriend walked through the door, ign   g him and smiling in Jan and Clare's direction. ard to believe that Ruth, who was so petite and pushing plain, had ever gone out with tall, handsome Ben Shipman. Putting them in the same shift was bound to be trouble. But Paul Grace had sanctioned it shortly before his death.

"It's good to be here," Ruth said.

Ben's jaw dropped.

Joe stood in a small shed, shivering. The shed was a temporary thing, erected by workmen who were busy converting the prison from high- to medium-security. Soon, all remand prisoners would be moved from Lincoln to Nottingham, saving the courts and the police a lot of travelling time. The prison population would double in a year. At the moment, though, the place resembled a building site. All sorts of stuff was stored inside. And there were plenty of places to hide.

It wasn't too late to go back, give himself up. He couldn't be charged with escaping, just hiding, which was hardly a serious offence.

Joe hadn't been convicted of anything yet. He was only on remand. At first, the police had offered to go soft on him. But when he refused to testify against the motorway team, they kept finding new burglaries to pin on him. They'd caught Joe's ex-partner in crime, Darren Braithwaite, and he was singing like the proverbial bird. Idiot! So Joe was facing serious time. Escaping would make it more serious.

But if Joe let the others down, and the escape failed, he would be to blame. And there were already enough people after him. Maybe this was the chance he'd been waiting for. He could team up with Griff, make a mint in the crack game. But Griff was keeping quiet, like he wished that Joe wasn't there. He would probably have some explaining to do when his mates on the out realized that there were three of them escaping, instead of two.

Gordon Loscoe looked at his watch.

"Is it time?" Griff whispered.

"Yeah. But we should be able to hear them coming. We don't want to be in the open any longer than necessary."

Then there was a rumbling outside, beyond the two tall prison walls. Grinning, Gordon got up.

"France, here I come!" he said.

Joe opened the shed door. Half of him expected a searchlight, guards everywhere. But there was only the sound of a lorry approaching. He looked back at the shadowed outline of the prison at night. The big clock, which the prison was built around, showed five past ten. Suddenly a ladder came flying over the double walls, landing with a heart-stopping clatter. Griff hurried to erect it. Joe helped. This was it! he realized, with a sense of shock, as no alarm went off, no men or dogs came rushing towards them. They were really going to escape.

The phone rang, a welcome distraction. Ben turned away from Ruth to answer it.

"Can you talk?"

The voice on the other end was Julie Wilder, the girl Ben had ditched Ruth for.

"Not really," he said.

They hadn't spoken for days. Less than two weeks ago, they had nearly slept together, but Julie had pulled back. Now neither of them knew where they stood.

"Are you coming off shift?" she asked.

"No, I just started."

"I really need to see you." Her voice sounded bleak, desperate.

"All right," Ben told her. "I'll see what I can do."

He put the phone down and turned to Jan Hunt, Ruth watching all the while.

"Sorry, Sarge, I need to take a little personal time."

"I thought you had all that paperwork," Jan teased him.

"It's important. Gary's on top of the court stuff."

"All right," Jan said. "Make sure you don't lean on him too much, though. You're his mentor, not the other way round."

"Thanks, Sarge."

Ben took one of the cars. Five minutes later he was knocking on Julie's door in the Maynard Estate.

"'S'open."

Julie was sitting on the sofa, her eyes puffy from crying. She wore a crumpled T-shirt and jeans. Curt, Julie's brother, was watching a film on Channel 5, but as Ben arrived, he clicked off the set and went upstairs. Curt didn't dislike Ben, but he didn't like policemen generally, and they never exchanged much conversation.

"What is it?" Ben asked. "Why did you call me at work?"

"I'm sorry," Julie said. "I left two messages on your machine but you didn't call back."

"I've been in Mansfield all day, visiting family."

He'd told them that he'd broken up with Ruth, but not that he'd been seeing a seventeen-year-old single mother from the city's roughest estate. After all, nothing might come of it. He and Julie hadn't even slept together yet. And Julie didn't know that

Ben had chucked Ruth. He didn't want her to think that she had that much power over him.

"Oh," Julie said. "Right. Family."

She pulled a letter from down the side of the sofa and passed it to Ben. It was postmarked Paris and addressed to both Julie and Curt. Ben didn't recognize the handwriting.

"You can read it if you want," Julie said.

Ben resisted. All along, he had avoided getting too close to Julie. He was mad about her, physically, but he also knew that she was trouble. Julie's whole family were trouble. Now and then he'd got useful information from her, but he didn't want to start reading her personal mail. He had no idea how he was going to explain their relationship – if it *was* a relationship – to his new boss, Tony Winter.

"Tell me."

"It's Mum. She's gone abroad with Eddie."

"I'd figured that out."

Julie's mother was the girlfriend of a member of the motorway team. Eddie Broom, believed to be the lookout man, had fled abroad rather than be questioned by the police about Paul Grace's murder. He'd taken Shirley, who was with him at the time, along for the ride.

"They're not coming back."

"*What?*"

"Mum's not coming back, ever. *Eddie says it's too risky.* That's all she says. Well, there's a bit about how she'll send some money when she can and the council should let me carry on the tenancy because of the baby. But she's not coming back. *Sorry*. That's all she says. *But I know you'll understand I couldn't miss this chance*."

Ben sat down and put his arms around her. "You'll get by," he said.

Julie began to cry. "I don't want to just *get by*," she said. "There's only me and Tammy now. Curt's neither use nor ornament. If the social find out Mum's gone they might take him into care anyway."

"They wouldn't manage to keep him long," Ben quipped, but Julie didn't smile.

"I'm too young," she told Ben. "I can't cope on my own."

She was exaggerating, he knew that. Julie was one of the most resourceful women he'd met. But tonight she was vulnerable and her tears could melt the iciest of hearts.

"You're not alone," he told her. "You've got me."

2

From the cabin of his lorry, Tim Jennings got a good look at Her Majesty's Prison. The gaol occupied an area the size of two football stadiums at the top end of Sherwood. Building work was going on at the front. Ladders and scaffolding almost obscured the sign warning visitors of what would happen if they helped a prisoner escape: a five-year sentence. The sign also gave warnings about the dire consequences of bringing in tobacco, alcohol or illegal drugs. The building work was being done to convert the prison from a high-security gaol into a medium-security one, holding more prisoners. The workers were behind schedule and extra men had been drafted in at short notice. Inevitably, security was less tight than usual.

The plan was simple. A JCB excavator had been stolen to order. A prison guard had left open a temporary hut which workmen had erected near the prison wall. The same guard had failed to spot the absence of three men from their beds during the evening roll check. The three missing men had been hiding in the hut at the edge of the sports field for several hours. By now they would be very cold.

Satisfied that all was normal, Tim had driven his lorry round the back and parked up. It had just turned ten, which was when the police shifts changed over. All of the squad cars returned to their stations, adding five minutes to their pursuit times – five minutes which made escape possible. The prison didn't have enough staff to give chase and, by the time the police got here, the prisoners would be long gone.

The two perimeter fences were six metres high, topped with big circles of barbed wire. Climbing to the top of them would be difficult, even with a six-metre ladder. Jumping over the barbed wire was virtually impossible. Should you manage that, however, there remained the problem of getting to the ground on the other side without breaking any bones. That was why they needed the JCB excavator.

At the rear of the prison was a small cul-de-sac called Gunthorpe Close. A couple of houses actually backed on to the prison wall. There was a triangular patch of land on each side of the houses. The larger one held a couple of allotments, the smaller was waste ground. The gap between the houses which led on to the waste ground was just big enough to drive a lorry across.

At five-past ten, Tim started the engine. He put the lorry into gear, then drove it down Gunthorpe Road, on to the Close, and over the kerb into the waste ground. Residents would be disturbed. Someone was bound to call the police. But it didn't matter. They had time. He'd made sure that the lorry was in exactly the right position.

As luck would have it, there was a full moon. The excavator, which ran on caterpillar tracks, would probably get over the rough ground on its own. But it was mounted on the lorry, making it high enough to reach over the wall. Tim heard Chris, in the JCB, switching the engine on. He watched as the excavator raised its bucket, then lowered it again. He saw Chris throw over the ladder. Moments later, a silhouette appeared above the wall. With difficulty, the first man clambered off the ladder and into the bucket of the excavator.

The second man was more of a youth, really. He climbed aboard easily. But the last man had more trouble. He was badly overweight and Chris had to lower the bucket a little further so that the others could help him climb inside.

The prison siren went off just as Tim began to back away. *Don't panic*, he told himself, turning the steering wheel. But that was easier said than done. The space for turning was tight and people had been using the waste land as a dumping ground. If he wasn't careful, he might back into an old fridge or a bit of car chassis. With the weight in the bucket, it would be easy to turn the lorry over. Tim moved forward and gave a glancing blow to one of the houses. *This is daft*, he decided. He braked and got out, running round to the back of the lorry, where the three escapees stood, shivering, in the excavator's big bucket.

"Car's at the end of the street!" he called to the occupants, who tumbled out, then ran towards the getaway vehicle.

Chris got out of the excavator and scrambled on to the waste ground. He and Tim ran to the getaway car, a big Japanese four-wheel-drive job, stolen earlier in the day. The prisoners were already under blankets. As Tim tore off his mask, Kevin drove away.

They didn't hit Hucknall Road and turn on to the ringroad, as the police would expect, but wove their way along the back streets of Sherwood, towards the city.

Gary Monk was typing up a report on a domestic assault in Radford while listening to the news up-date on Radio 5.

"Nottingham Forest have accepted a fee of £750,000

for their young striker, Dean Sutherland. This marks a five hundred thousand-pound profit in five months for the club, but still represents a bargain basement price for the young goal scorer, who makes a surprise move to Scottish club, Motherwell. Rumours of impending criminal charges for the player have been denied by his agent…"

Gary turned off the radio. He already knew the full story from his boyfriend, Umberto, who was a Forest first team regular. After his recent humiliating experiences, Dean wanted to get as far away from Nottingham as possible. And who could blame him?

The phone rang and Gary picked it up. Oxclose Lane Station.

"We've had an escape from the prison."

"When?"

"Reported three minutes ago."

"How many men?" Gary asked.

"Don't know yet, but we want all available cars into the area around the prison straight away. They'll be searching the side streets or forming road blocks."

"I'm on to it," Gary said.

He put down the phone then picked it up again. Jan, Clare, Ruth and John were already in cars, so would have received the message. The person he needed to get through to was Ben, who was out in the shift's third car. His partner hadn't told him where he was going, but Gary had a pretty good idea. Lately, when Ben got that distant look in his eyes, it meant that he was seeing Julie Wilder.

Gary thought that Ben was mad, making moves on a girl like that. Sure, she was pretty, and nice enough, maybe, when isolated from the rest of her family. But she was also an accident waiting to happen. The accident could happen tonight, if Ben didn't get over here in that car, pronto.

As Gary radioed his mentor, Inspector Winter charged into the parade room.

"What are you still doing here, man? Haven't you heard what's going on?"

"I'm on my way, boss," Gary said, hoping that the Inspector was too wired to wait and see who he was calling.

"First escape in years, this," Winter said, as he grabbed a radio at the door and headed out. "A lot of us said there'd be trouble when they decided to expand the numbers at the nick. There'll be hell to pay if we don't get them tonight."

"I'm sure we will," Gary said, waiting for Ben's voice on the line. What the hell was he playing at? *Get your pants back on and answer, you idiot!* he shouted silently, as the Inspector yelled, mercifully: "I'm taking my own car. I'll be at Oxclose Lane, if anyone needs me."

Still, Ben didn't answer. Did Julie Wilder have a phone? She must, if it was her who'd called a few minutes ago. Cursing his partner, Gary called directory enquiries, then dialled Julie's number. The line was engaged.

"Is there any more information about the escape?" Jan asked, as she and Clare sped towards Sherwood.

The radio replied. "*According to a witness, at least two men got over a wall with help from a crane mounted on a lorry. The escapees and their helpers then transferred to a newish Jap four-wheel-drive, dark colour.*"

"Is the helicopter on to it?"

The county had recently bought a twin-engined Squirrel helicopter. It was shared with Derbyshire and based in Ripley, twenty or so miles away. It had heat-seeking devices which meant that it could not only follow cars, but also track criminals in the dark – even when they were hiding in bushes, or inside a building.

"*It's out of action, being serviced. But roadblocks are being put into place.*"

"I see. Thanks." Jan had little faith in roadblocks. This sounded like a professional escape. Chances were, the escapers would be out of the county before any of these measures made any difference.

"Let's get on to the Hucknall Road and the streets around the prison," she told Clare. Jan knew those roads, having lived round there for a while when Kevin was working at the City Hospital.

"They'll be halfway to the motorway by now, won't they?" Clare said.

"They'll probably find somewhere to switch vehicles first," Jan argued.

"It would help if we knew who we were looking for," Clare said.

"Yes," Jan told her, "it would."

The car didn't go far – didn't even, as far as Joe could tell, hit the main road. The driver told them they could get out from under the blankets and Joe looked around. They were on a deserted side street. If Joe was any judge of distance, they could only be a few minute's walk from the prison. It was very risky. There were three men in the front of the four-wheel drive. One of them was holding a powerful flashlight, which he shone at Joe, blinding him.

"Out you get!" Joe did as he was told.

Gordon Loscoe stood next to him. The million-aire didn't look like a rich man, more like a market stall owner. However, he'd won the Lottery, so he must have a big wad stashed away somewhere. Now the driver tossed him some keys.

"Your car's just up the road, Gordon. A blue Sierra. Know where you're going?"

Gordon Loscoe nodded.

"Your passport and tickets are in the glove compartment. Some cash, too. Eddie says hi and he'll meet you at the other end."

Loscoe smiled sheepishly. "See you," he said. "And thanks."

The driver turned to Griff. "Off you go, too."

"Here?" Griff said, incredulous. "We're only five minutes from the prison!"

"The deal was we got you out, not took you to a hotel. Tell you what…" He got some change out of his pocket and handed it to Griff. "Buses are still running."

Disturbed, Joe looked at Griff. "Shall I come with you?" he asked, imploringly. Griff was bound to have somewhere to go. Joe didn't.

Griff looked away without replying, then began to jog, down the street, around the corner, and out of sight.

"Back in the car," the driver told Joe.

"What do you want with me?" Joe asked. "I'm not even supposed to be here!"

"Just do as you're told."

Joe did. They drove past Griff, who was now running awkwardly, his head constantly jerking around to see if he was being watched. The three men in the car laughed.

"He won't last five minutes," the driver said.

Joe caught the name of the road as they turned on to it: Caledon. The car entered a wide driveway, parking out of sight from the street.

"Move the other car," the driver instructed one of the others, then turned to Joe.

"Got something for you, in the garage."

He got out of the car. Nothing felt right. Alone

for a moment, Joe had to think quickly. The flashlight had been left in the car's side pocket. He snatched it before getting out and stuffed it inside his baggy shirt.

As the garage door opened, Joe remembered who the other guy was – the younger one who'd been driving the lorry. That night, two weeks ago, his attention had been more focused on his boss, Chris. The garage light went on.

"This wasn't to get Loscoe out," Joe told the driver, sensing the other one coming up behind him. "This was to get me."

"Correct," said the third man, grabbing his shoulder. Joe knew his name: Christopher Stevens. He was the motorway team's leader. And he was holding a gun.

"I'd never have testified against you," Joe said. "You've got to believe me. I—"

"We don't believe in taking risks," Stevens said, pointing the gun at him. "You were in the wrong place at the wrong time, Sunny Jim. You're dead."

3

Reports rang from the radio, none of them rewarding or reassuring. Oxclose Lane station, on the other side of the prison, had sent cars to the motorway. Four-wheel-drives of every kind were being stopped. Still there was no description of the escaped prisoners, much less names. Jan drove slowly around the Sherwood streets.

"They're long gone," Clare said.

"We still have to check."

"They used a crane!" Clare protested. "This is a well planned, well resourced operation. They're probably in a safe house somewhere, waiting it out."

"Probably," Jan agreed.

A car was coming down Victoria Road. Clare looked at the driver just as he glanced at her. He bore a striking resemblance to Gordon Loscoe, the former Lottery millionaire, currently residing in the prison up the road.

"Look at him," Clare told Jan, but the sergeant didn't know Loscoe, and the face meant nothing to her.

"Wonder who's on night crime duty," the sergeant said. "They should be over at the prison by now."

"Depends where they've had to come from," Clare commented.

Night crime duty only came up a couple of times a year. When it was your turn, you had to cover a huge area, from the city over to Hucknall. Clare had been with CID for a few weeks, but never pulled a night crime duty, not officially. After Paul died, she would have liked to stay in CID. If possible, she would have liked to help investigate his death. But CID only took Clare on as a favour to Paul, because he hadn't wanted his girlfriend working in the shift that he supervised.

This morning, DI Greasby had called Clare into his office and asked her whether she wanted to take some more time off.

"Work's the only thing that'll keep me sane," she'd told him.

"I can understand that," the Inspector said. "Routine's important. However, no one expects you to be able to give a hundred per cent, not as things stand."

"It'll be easier once we catch—"

"*If*," the DI corrected her. "I want you to go to counselling."

"I'd rather not." Counselling didn't look good on an officer's record, no matter how much the top brass denied it.

"I can't force you," the DI said, "but, for now, I'm putting you back in uniform. I've already had Tony Winter wanting to know why you're still on placement with us."

Clare flinched but didn't show emotion. She had to prove that she was strong enough to carry on. "My understanding was that I could see out my probation in CID," she'd said in a cold voice, remembering in time to add the word "sir".

"That would have been very unusual," Greasby told her. "You'll make a good detective, Clare. When your probation's up, I'll have you back with pleasure. But there are procedures to follow…"

So here she was, back in the shift where she'd started out, the one that Paul used to be in charge of. Not too tactful, that. But tact and diplomacy were never the force's strong suit.

"This is getting us nowhere," Jan said. "Who was that bloke you recognized?" Clare told her. But it couldn't have been Loscoe, could it? The car was all wrong and, anyway, he wasn't the escaping kind.

The front gate at the prison was "frozen", which

meant that only police officers and prison officials could get through. There was a sign in front of the desk, and someone was writing on it as Neil entered. There were three sections. The first two listed men out in hospital or on home visits. The third looked like this:

UNLAWFULLY AT LARGE

NO	NAME	COMMENTS
139	Loscoe, Gordon	
158	Griffiths, Brett	
607	~~Hatton, Joseph~~	Remand

Neil showed his warrant card and the officer on duty waved him into the cage, which locked behind him. Once Neil had been cleared, the door on the other side clicked open and he was met by one of the deputy governors, a brown-haired man with heavy glasses and a serious smile.

"Are you the CID liaison officer?" he asked Neil.

"No. I'm the Night Crime officer. Oxclose Lane are raising the liaison officer at the moment."

"I'm Roger Garton. The Silver Commander's on her way over, but I've already set up the Escape Incident Suite."

"Good."

"Silver Commander" was police code for the governor. Neil followed Garton through the dark to the old building in the centre of the prison. The administration offices were at the edge of the building. Beyond them was the old block, which used to house lifers, but now contained prisoners doing five years or less.

"Where did they go from?" Neil asked.

"Here. Or rather, they should have come back here. They hid in a hut on the edge of the prison complex."

"And nobody missed them?"

The deputy governor sighed. "Now, therein lies a story."

He took Neil into the Incident Suite, which was the governor's office. A clock on the wall showed 22.14. Beneath it sat a white-haired man. He looked like somebody's grandfather, like he ought to be on a pension. He looked like he was at his own funeral.

"This is Arthur Evans. He did the roll check this evening. Tell this chap, Arthur."

The haunted look on the man's face would stay with Neil for a long time.

"They've got my wife," he said. "I got a phone call and they put Joanne on the line. She said they were going to kill her if I didn't do what they said."

Neil turned to Garton.

"His wife, Joanne. Is she…?"

"I was just about to call Oxclose Lane. They live nearby, in Mapperley."

"And the three men who've gone?"

"Two were sharing a cell on the ground floor. The other was on the third floor, doing five years."

They were interrupted by the arrival of the Prison Governor. Elizabeth Teale was a slender woman in her early forties.

"You're younger than I expected," she said.

"My boss'll be out soon. And his boss, too," Neil told her. *Just as soon as they're dragged out of the pub*, he could have added. "In the meantime, I'm on duty. I see you've identified the escapers."

"Yes. Three men. Gordon Loscoe, 35. He's—"

"I know who he is. The others?"

"Joe Hatton, 18. He's on remand for—"

An alarm bell rang in Neil's head. "I know about that, too," he said.

"The last one's Brett Griffiths, 22." When Neil was silent, she added, sarcastically, "It can't be that you don't know every single one of my inmates, can it?"

Neil smiled. "What's he in for?"

"Dealing rock cocaine at a nightclub in the city. Small fry. Your lot have been trying to get him to give evidence against his boss, the nightclub owner."

Neil radioed the names and descriptions of the escapees, then explained about Joanne Evans. The governor looked shocked. It was clearly the first she'd heard of it.

"I'd better talk to Arthur," she told Neil.

"Officers should be at their house in a couple of minutes," Neil said. He doubted that any of the men who'd threatened Mrs Evans would still be there.

* * *

"*Escaped convicts have now been identified as…*"

Clare listened to the report and groaned when Gordon Loscoe's name came up. She was in trouble.

"I thought you said he wasn't the escaping kind," Jan commented.

"I was sure—"

"What colour was the car?" Jan asked, interrupting.

"Black. No, blue. Dark blue, I think. A Sierra."

"Do you remember any of the licence plate?"

"No," Clare snapped. "Do you?"

"I'm not the one recognized him," Jan said as she radioed in the details of Loscoe's car.

"What I don't understand," Clare said, "is how come he was on his own, so soon after the escape."

"Good planning," Jan told her. "Now, what about the other two? Loscoe's got money, but most convicts haven't. What's the betting they're still around?"

"I'm not very good at calculating odds," Clare said, as they began yet another sweep of the area. She found herself remembering her two trips to the casino with Paul. Both times, they'd won. Thinking about Paul made Clare miserable. She should have been in Paris with him this last weekend, buying an engagement ring. Instead, she'd buried him. No one knew. That was almost the worst thing. No one knew that Paul and Clare were going to be married.

Even Paul hadn't known it, because she'd turned him down and he'd died before Clare could tell him that she'd changed her mind.

So, at the funeral, Clare was only "the girl-friend", which wasn't the same as being a fiancée. Should she have told people that he'd asked her to marry him? His being dead seemed bad enough. She hadn't seen the point of making her bereavement even worse. The one person who Clare would normally have confided in was Ruth. But Clare's best friend had just lost her own boyfriend. Ben had dropped Ruth like a used sweet wrapper, with no explanation and little apology. Their twin disasters had separated the friends. Neither could think of the right words to comfort the other.

At the funeral, Paul's parents hardly talked to Clare. She had driven to Berkshire, with Gary and Ben, in uniform, as was proper. The chief constable was there too, and he introduced Clare as "your son's young lady", but Mr and Mrs Grace made no special effort to talk to her. The four officers were invited back to the house afterwards. Clare wanted to see the place where Paul grew up. She would have liked to see the family album, but it wasn't offered, so she had to content herself with staring at a photo of Paul aged ten, holding a trophy which he'd received for winning a junior chess championship. They didn't stay long.

This morning, she'd gone to his maisonette in

Arnold, meaning to say a last goodbye, pick up the few things she'd left there, maybe take something small away with her, as a keepsake. It was the first time she'd summoned up the nerve to go to his house since it happened. After all, this was the place where they'd made love for the first time. This was the place outside which he'd been shot and killed. But Clare needn't have worried about memories messing with her mind. The house had been cleaned out completely. All trace of Paul was gone.

In the job, though, there were constant reminders. Clare kept imagining that Paul would appear at any moment. His voice would be the next one she heard on the radio. She'd hurried to return to work without really reckoning on that. If she wanted to get over Paul, Clare realized, she might have to leave the force altogether.

"You messed up our retirement," the balding one said. "One more big job and we were done. Now the police know who all of us are, so we have to leave the country, thanks to you."

"Get it over with," the voice behind Joe said.

Joe could guess what was coming and his mind went into overdrive. The one behind him hadn't locked the garage door. It was his only chance.

"I wasn't to know that you'd do the footballer's house the same night we did," he whinged. It had seemed such a lucky break, getting into the riverside house of the rich footballer. Lucky, that was, until the armed men broke in after him. They'd come for a bunch of paintings which Joe didn't even want.

"Did you kill him?" he asked the bald one. "That policeman?"

Stevens laughed. "I was in the nick at the time. We all were. But I'm going to kill you."

"Hold on," said the other one, the youngest of the three. "I thought we agreed…"

"Shut it, Tim."

The one called Tim looked angry. He was exchanging a glance with the one behind Joe. It was time to seize the moment.

"Go ahead, then," Joe said to Stevens, the one with the shooter in his hand. "Do it."

That threw them for a second. Joe took a step back. He pulled the flashlight from out of his shirt. The driver had used it to dazzle Joe earlier, to make sure that he didn't recognize them until it was too late. Now it might buy Joe another second or two.

"What are you going to do with that?" Stevens said, laughing. "Morse code?"

Joe reached to his side and switched off the garage light.

"You stupid toe-rag!" Stevens said, as they were plunged into darkness.

Joe kicked the door open, and crashed out of the garage. He couldn't believe his luck. A car was waiting at the end of the drive, its engine running. As the men ran out of the garage after him, Joe turned the flashlight on. He put on his deepest, loudest, voice.

"Police! Freeze!" he yelled. That stopped them for a moment. Joe opened the car door, threw the flashlight at the men, and jumped in.

His trick had only gained him a few metres. Now a gun pointed at the window. Joe pushed the central locking device down, ignoring the weapon. Fear for his life made his mind crystal clear. The team wouldn't want a gunshot to draw attention to themselves, not with so many police around. The dashboard clock read 22.18. Joe put his foot down on the biggest pedal. The car was an automatic. It sailed out into the road, with the three stranded members of the motorway team standing impotently behind it.

4

"*Mrs Evans is being held against her will in her home at number seven, Hancock Rise, Mapperley. Proceed with caution and request armed back-up if there is any possibility that her assailants are still present.*"

"I don't know Mapperley," Ruth told John. "Do you?"

"It's where I live," Farraday told her, then spoke into the radio. "3704 responding." They sped along the Woodborough Road. "We'll probably be the third or fourth car on the scene," he told Ruth.

He was wrong. Hancock Rise was quiet. The curtains in well-to-do houses were closed, with only muted light behind them: the world and his wife watching television. There were no lights on at number seven, no signs of life whatsoever.

"Whoever held her hostage," Ruth said, "they're long gone."

"Probably," John told her. "But we don't know what state Mrs Evans is in. She could be dead, tied up, or booby-trapped in some way. I'm going to take a look round the back."

"I'll come with you," Ruth said, adding, "It's not a good idea for us to get separated."

The back of the semi-detached house was as dark as the front.

"Ever had a situation like this before?" Ruth asked John.

"Not since I retired from the SAS."

"You were in the SAS?"

John frowned at her. "Joke." He tried the back door. It was locked. Ruth radioed Oxclose Lane. "We're going in."

"We should wait for back-up," John said.

"And what if she dies of suffocation or a heart attack during the next five minutes?"

"You've got a point," John conceded, and used his truncheon to smash the glass above the back door. There was a key in it. Ruth wrapped her hand in a handkerchief, reached in, and turned it.

"Police!" she called out, as they opened the door and stumbled into the dark kitchen. "Don't worry, Mrs Evans, we're here to help you."

The three members of the motorway team stood

outside the garage on Caledon Road.

"I say we go after him," Kevin Hunter said.

"In the four-wheeler?" Chris replied in a mocking tone. "We'll be arrested in minutes. I can't believe you let him go."

"I can't believe you didn't shoot him," Kevin said.

Tim kept quiet. He had known these men all his adult life. But he had always been the runt: four years younger than Kevin, six years younger than Chris, who he'd met in prison. In theory, Tim was an equal part of the team. But only in theory.

"I've never had to shoot anyone in my life," Chris said.

"I had the car running and everything." Kevin.

"That's you all over." Chris. "Leaving the keys in the car! It never occurred to you that someone might nick it, did it?"

"It was in the sodding drive!" Kevin protested.

"Same as it never occurred to you to cosh that Inspector when he caught you in the car. If you'd got him then, we'd have got away, wouldn't we?"

Kevin sighed. "Not that again!"

And they wouldn't have needed to kill him, either, Tim thought. Half a lifetime as a professional criminal and he'd never done more than hit someone on the head. Now he was partly responsible for one death and, had Chris not screwed up, would have been in on another, too. The others had lied to him about what they planned to do with Joe.

"What if Hatton goes to the police," Tim interrupted, speaking for the first time, "tells them that we're here?"

The other two stopped bickering.

"You've got a point," Chris said, and got out his mobile. "I'll call a taxi."

"One small problem," Kevin pointed out. "Where are we going?"

"We can't do this," Ben said, "not now." They were half undressed on the sofa. Neither of them had meant this to happen, but they'd got carried away. As Ben did up his shirt, Julie felt embarrassed, cheap.

"I'm sorry," Ben said, adding, unnecessarily, "I'm on duty."

"It's OK," Julie told him. "I don't want it to happen like this. I want..." She let the sentence trail off, afraid to tell the truth. Julie wanted wine, moonlight, flowers ... she wanted all the things she imagined Mum getting in the South of France.

"What time is it?"

"Just gone twenty-past."

"I'll just radio that I'm on my way back."

He picked up the device and cursed.

"What is it?" Julie asked.

"I was in a hurry to come here and didn't check the battery. It's dead. Can I use the phone?"

"Sure."

"It's off the hook."

"Tammy does that sometimes," Julie explained, as he dialled. Actually, she had taken the phone off the hook earlier, when Ben knocked on the door. She hadn't wanted them disturbed by anything.

"There's been a what?" Ben sounded half angry, half nervous. "I'm on my way."

"What's happening?" Julie asked him.

"Prison escape. I've got to go." He swore again. "I shouldn't have come."

"I'm glad you did," Julie said. She almost added, "I needed you," but he already knew how vulnerable she was. Julie didn't want to rub it in. Ben kissed her.

"If you like, I could come by later, when my shift ends."

"I'd like that," Julie said.

He hurried out. Julie felt a wave of relief. He was coming back. Every time she saw Ben Shipman, she was sure that she was going to scare him off. But it hadn't happened yet. The phone began to ring, interrupting her reverie. Julie answered it.

"Is Shirley there?" That was Mum's first name.

"No," Julie said. The man at the other end swore. She recognized his voice.

"When'll she be back?"

"I don't know."

Officially, if the dole asked, or the school people, Shirley had gone away for a few days.

"Is this Natalie's dad?" Julie asked, cagily.

A sigh. "Yeah, that's right, Julie love."

"Do they let you make phone calls at this time?"

"I'm out."

"*What?*" Julie connected the dots between this conversation and what Ben had just told her about the prison escape.

"Look, I just wanted Shirley to get a message to Natalie and Maxine. I can't call the house. They'll be tracing the calls."

Maxine was Gordon Loscoe's wife. "What message?" Julie asked.

"I'll send for them when I'm sorted. All right?"

"I'll pass it on," Julie said.

"Gotta go."

He hung up. Julie could have done without this grief. But Gordon wasn't to know that her boyfriend was a policeman. She went up to tell her brother about the call.

"You're kidding!" Curt said. "I have to ring Nat."

"No way," Julie said. "Gordon told me that the police'll be tracing the calls. Anyway, they're probably round there already."

"Let's go and watch it on the news, then."

They went downstairs and put on the closing moments of "News at Ten", waiting for the local news section which came on afterwards. They watched it all, but there was no report about the escape.

* * *

The prison guard's house was silent but for the ticking of a clock in the hall.

"They might have taken her somewhere else," John said.

Or they might have killed her, Ruth thought, but didn't say. She groped for light switches, then opened a door. The neat dining room was dominated by a circular oak table. You could smell the polish. No one there. The living room was empty, too. The clock on the video recorder flashed 22:29.

"Upstairs," John said, as another car pulled up outside. Without waiting for reinforcements, Ruth followed him.

They heard her thrashing about before they even opened the bedroom door. Joanne Evans had her hands tied behind her back and her ankles strapped together. She was also gagged. Ruth removed the gag while John let in the new arrivals.

"It's all right," she told the prison guard's wife. "Everything's all right."

"Arthur..." was the first word she said.

"He's fine. But he's worried about you. Did they hurt you?"

"Not really."

"Can you describe them?"

Joanne nodded vigorously. "I've been thinking about nothing else for the last few hours. One of them's nearly bald. He was wearing..."

* * *

Tim Jennings listened to Chris and Kevin arguing. Everything had come unstuck. Not only had Joe got away in Kevin's car, but it was his legitimate car, the one registered in his name. If the police caught Joe in it, the escape would have the opposite effect to the one intended. Joe would talk to the police, rather than risk having his sentence extended for escaping. What choice did he have, now that he knew the team were willing to kill him? Tim still reckoned that paying him off would have been a better bet.

After phoning for a taxi, Chris made a call to their contact and explained the situation.

"He needs taking out. Help us get him and we'll see you right, for good."

The taxi arrived. Chris asked to be taken to the West Bridgford pub where the others' cars were parked. Either Tim or Chris would have to take Kevin home with them – Kevin couldn't go back to his own gaff in case the police were already on to him.

None of these calculations were discussed in the taxi. The three men sat in silence, wondering how they'd got into this situation. A month ago, they'd made their pile. Each had millions stashed away. But they were becoming too famous. The police were getting embarrassed. They threw so many resources into tracking down the team that, sooner or later, they were bound to catch them. After the

Loscoe fiasco, Eddie wanted to retire then and there. Chris proposed that they go out on one final mega-job. Big mistake. For years they'd been magic, untouchable. These last two weeks, that safe feeling had dissolved. Tonight, the three of them together couldn't take out an eighteen-year-old.

The taxi driver dropped them at the pub and grunted thanks for the one-pound tip. They got out and, instead of going in, walked across the car park.

"I don't believe it!" Chris shouted. "I don't!"

His car had been broken into. The passenger-side window was smashed. Chris had a stereo with a removable face, so there was nothing to nick. The thieves had smashed up the base unit anyway. Then they'd had a go at scarfing the steering column. Loose wires poured out of it. Chris tried the key in the ignition. It wouldn't start.

"I'll have a go," Kevin said. He was the one who always nicked the cars, as well as driving them. He fiddled with the ignition, poked a screwdriver in the steering column. No joy. All the time this was going on, Chris could be heard swearing. A couple of people coming out of the pub watched him at it.

"Bad do, mate," one of them said, and was frightened away by Chris's angry stare.

Chris was going psychotic, Tim decided, as the older man began to kick an Allegro which was parked alongside the Rover. Tim wanted to tell him to calm down. He was drawing attention to himself.

But he couldn't talk to Chris when he was in this state. Tim was glad that he was getting out of this. He was almost glad that the kid had got away.

"Any luck?" he asked Kevin, walking around the other side of the Rover in order to put as much distance between him and Chris as possible.

"Nope," Kevin said. "It's completely knackered."

It was only as Chris began to rant that Tim noticed the final indignity – the big, official notice stuck across the front windscreen of the car, the sad sign which told observers not to bother officialdom by reporting the crime because they already knew all about it.

The notice read: *POLICE AWARE*.

5

"Call for you," the Deputy Governor told Neil as he finished going through the escaped prisoners' files. It was Phil Church, Nottingham CID's liaison from the task force investigating the motorway team.

"Didn't take you long," Neil said.

"Joe Hatton is the best witness we've got," Church told him. "We've been piling pressure on him to testify against Stevens and Jennings in court."

"Congratulations," Neil said. "It looks like you put on enough pressure to persuade him to do a runner."

"Are you the most senior officer there?" Church asked.

"Both the CID Liaison officer and DI Greasby are on their way," Neil said, unapologetically.

"And so am I. I've spoken to DCI Charlton." Chief Inspector Charlton was in charge of the task force.

"He and I are coming over. If you pick up Hatton, we want to interview him straight away. He may be ready to crack."

"Fair enough," Neil said. "See you in an hour or so."

He put the phone down and resumed looking at the files. If he could find something before the more senior officers got here, it would be a feather in his cap. And if Church was right and this was connected to the motorway team, then maybe he'd find something which would lead to Paul Grace's killer.

The Inspector's death had been the main preoccupation of CID for the past two weeks. Neil was one of the last people to see Paul Grace alive. It felt weird. Neil had just got used to Grace going out with Clare, his ex. Now Grace was gone and Neil didn't know how to deal with Clare. He'd sent her a note – *if there's anything I can do* – but she'd been off work, so he hadn't seen her. He felt hopeless. When Angelo, Clare's brother, died, Neil had been there for her. He wanted to help her now, but didn't know how to. The best he could do for her was to help catch her boyfriend's killer.

Paul Grace had thought that the motorway team used a police informant, someone they bribed to find out the state of the police's investigation. But there was no evidence to back the idea up, only hunches. Neil meant to discuss the theory with Clare when they next got together – *if* they got together. It was hard, being friends with an ex, even before Grace's death. But Neil had far more in common with Clare than he did with his current girlfriend, who was a second-year student at Trent University. He missed her.

"Rendezvous at Oxclose Lane in five minutes," Clare and Jan were told over the radio. "Inspector Winter will be waiting for you."

Clare wasn't looking forward to seeing Winter. She hated having egg on her face. Back on the job for five minutes, she'd let an escaped prisoner drive past her. Gary got a message on his radio. It was Ben.

"Where are you?"

"We're combing Sherwood, looking for escaped prisoners. I tried to call you."

"Sorry. There was a fault with my radio."

Clare, listening in the front seat, thought she knew a fib when she heard one. What had Ben been up to?

"We're on our way to Oxclose Lane," Gary told him. "Meet you there. Be as quick as you can, though. The boss is waiting for us."

"I'm on my way," Ben said.

Clare was curious about Tony Winter. "What do

you reckon to the new boss?" she asked the others. Jan was diplomatically silent.

"He's a boss," Gary said. "Seems to know his job. Bit distant, like, but then most of them are."

"Do *you* like him?" Clare asked Jan as they pulled into the car park at Oxclose Lane.

"I haven't decided yet," Jan said as they got out of the car. "But here he is. You'll have to make up your own mind."

Tony Winter stepped out of the shadows, a small man whose uniform made him look a little over-weight. How hard would he be on her? Clare decided to jump straight in with her confession.

"We think we saw Loscoe, but let him get away," Clare said. "It was before we knew he was one of the escapers."

As they walked into the station, she gave Winter the embarrassing details.

"We all make mistakes," he told her. "Anyway, Loscoe's not the priority tonight. Hatton is."

"Any idea where he's likely to be?" Jan asked.

"If those three have any sense, they split up as soon as they could. We've got officers waiting outside Hatton's mum's place in Mansfield to see if he shows up there. Gary and … where's Ben?"

"He'll be here in a minute," Gary said.

"I want you two to see that footballer mate of his in case he tries his luck with him. But as far as we can tell, Joe doesn't have any place to go. Someone from CID's at the prison now, asking around to see if anybody there knows something we don't."

"What do you want us to do?" Jan.

"Go back to your normal beat, but be ready to be pulled off any time. And keep an eye out for anything that might point to Hatton. According to the files, there's a squat he used a while back."

"It's been sold now," Jan said. "A building association are doing it up."

"He still might use it for the night. He hasn't got anywhere else to go."

Ben rushed into the foyer, looking sweaty and out of breath.

"I'll brief you," Gary said, before Winter could comment. "Come on."

Dean Sutherland had a short-term let in one of the posh new flats next to the river, a short walk from the City ground. Several other players had flats in the same complex.

"What are *you* doing here?" Dean asked, fear in his eyes, when he answered the door to Ben and Gary. He was still waiting to hear if the Crown Prosecution Service were going to bring charges against him for his part in the burglary at Umberto's house. He'd been blackmailed into helping set up the burglary. If Dean was charged, it might mess up his transfer to Motherwell.

"Can we come in?" Ben asked.

"Must you?"

"Who is it, Dean?" a female voice called from the bedroom.

"Just a minute, Karen."

"Seen Joe Hatton lately?" Gary asked, in a pointed voice. Dean was Joe's oldest friend.

"I've not been doing any prison visiting, no."

"Thing is," Ben said, "Joe's escaped. We thought he might come here."

"*Escaped?*" That threw Dean for a moment. "No, no, he doesn't know my address."

"If he gets in touch, we want you to call," Ben said. "Immediately, OK?"

"OK. Sure."

"Dean, what's going on?" The girl's voice again.

"Just coming," Dean yelled, then told the officers, "I'll call, I promise. But he won't come here."

"Believe him?" Gary asked, as they left the complex.

"Hard to tell. He and Joe go back a long way," Ben said.

"Where to now?" Gary asked the Inspector over the radio.

"Try the Loscoe house. We had someone round there earlier, but nobody was in."

"You think Gordon Loscoe will go home?"

"No," Winter said. "He's more likely to phone, so we've put a trace on. But you never know, his wife might have something useful to tell us."

"So," Gary said as they drove back towards the city, "are you going to tell me where you were earlier?"

Ben hesitated, "I got a call from Julie Wilder, thought she might have some information about Eddie Broom, so I went over there."

"You said it was personal," Gary commented.

Ben stared at the road ahead as he spoke. "I wanted to see her alone, thought I'd get more that way."

I'll bet! Gary thought. "And?" was all he said.

"Her mum's gone."

"Where?"

"She's left the country. Gone to live with Eddie Broom in France. You know what that implies?"

Gary thought for a moment. Eddie Broom was the motorway team's reconnaissance man. If he'd moved abroad, it could only mean one thing.

"They've retired," he said.

"Looks like it. If Eddie's gone, the others are probably gone too."

"Unless they stayed behind to tidy up some loose ends."

Ben nodded and began to drive. Gary thought about Eddie Broom. Since he was the only member of the motorway team not in custody, he had been the first suspect questioned about Paul Grace's murder. But he had been in Scotland at the time. Shirley Wilder had confirmed this, as had DC Church from the Birmingham CID task force.

After Grace's death, the evidence against the three other members of the team became scanty. They hadn't actually been caught burgling Umberto Capricio's house, but were picked up near it. The three men's story was that they had parked on a side road then gone for a drink at the Trent Bridge Inn. Walking back along the river, they had separated and two of them had mistaken the road, overshot it. The one who'd got the right road, Kevin Hunter, was spotted waiting in his car by Paul Grace. Hunter's story was that he did a runner, not because he was involved in a burglary, but because he was over the limit and didn't want to get done for drunken driving.

As fairy stories went, this one was almost plausible, though you'd be pushed to explain why three men from different parts of the country got together to go for a drink in Nottingham on a Saturday night. However, without Paul Grace or Joe Hatton to say that they'd seen two of them in the act of committing a crime, the police had no case.

Ben pulled up outside the Loscoe household. It wasn't the mansion on the edge of the city which they used to occupy. Maxine and Natalie now lived in a three-bedroomed apartment in the cheaper end of Mapperley Park, not far from Ben's own rented flat. There were no lights on in the first-floor apartment, but that didn't mean anything. They could be in the back. Ben climbed a small set of stairs and rang the bell. Gary waited at the bottom in case Gordon Loscoe was in and tried to jump out of a window or do something equally stupid.

When no one answered the bell, Ben rang it again. Eventually, he heard footsteps. The door was opened, on the chain, by a fourteen-year-old girl who he recognized as Natalie Loscoe.

"Your mum in?" he enquired, politely.

Natalie shook her head. "You're Julie's boyfriend, aren't you?"

Ben frowned and didn't reply. Gary enjoyed his discomfort.

"Ben something?" Natalie asked.

"Yes, that's me. Have you heard from your dad tonight?"

"They don't let him make many phone calls where he is."

"I don't mean a phone call. He's escaped."

Natalie's eyes opened wide. "You're kidding!"

"I'm not kidding. You mean you didn't know?"

"My dad isn't clever enough to plan an escape. Are you sure it was him?"

"Where's your mum?" Ben continued.

"I don't know. I've only just got home myself. School trip to see 'Romeo and Juliet'."

"You must have some idea where Maxine's gone."

"She's not with my dad, if that's what you're thinking. I think she's got a new boyfriend."

If that was true, Maxine hadn't wasted any time. Gordon had only been inside for three weeks.

"I need his name, address."

"I don't know, do I?" Natalie protested.

"Listen," Ben said, leaning forward confidentially. "You dad's paid someone to get him out of prison and the money has to have been channelled through your mum. We need to know where she is."

Natalie shrugged. "Most nights she comes home just after midnight. Wakes me up, like you did. But you're barking up the wrong tree. We've hardly got any money, not until the other house sale goes through. And Mum doesn't want Dad out of prison, she's talking about divorcing him. Sorry."

Ben gave up. He wrote a note, asking Maxine to call as soon as she got in, then he rejoined Gary. "Hear all that?" he asked.

"I certainly did. So who's this Julie you're going out with, as if I couldn't guess?"

6

The car clock said 22:47. Joe didn't know where to go. He was from Mansfield, not Nottingham. But it was too risky to head for a hiding place in his home town. So he crashed across the ringroad and drove into the Bestwood Estate. Too many police cars on the ringroad. They might not have his car's make or licence-plate number, but they had his description, and he was still wearing prison clothes. He couldn't risk driving on major thoroughfares.

The Bestwood Estate, however, was full of speed bumps, designed to deter joy riders. Joe needed to stop somewhere, check out what was in the car and, if necessary, do a little thieving, but this wasn't the place. The speed bumps and boarded-up shops testified that this estate was full of thieves like him. He needed somewhere wealthier.

Joe cut on to Beckhampton Road, then along Chippenham. So far, so good. Fewer police than normal on this estate, probably because of the gaol break. He swerved down Bower, then realized that he was heading back for the ringroad. There was a brown sign saying something about a park (Joe didn't read too well). It pointed left. Joe turned up Bestwood Lodge Drive.

The drive was a long one. The road grew quieter as the houses grew smarter. Joe was glad that he was in a posh car, because it wouldn't look out of place if he parked round here. At the end of the drive the road seemed to head on into wilderness. Then he noticed a car park on the right. There were more houses if he turned left, isolated houses, easy to burgle. Joe looked at the clock on the dashboard. Half eleven. Bad time to do a burglary. Not everyone was asleep by then. If people were out, at the pub or whatever, they would be back soon. Maybe he ought to leave it for a while. Joe didn't want to take unnecessary risks, end up back inside before the night was over. Also, he'd never done a burglary without a look-out, and these houses were likely to have alarms. He'd better think it through, first. He drove ahead.

Joe had no idea where he was. This didn't feel anything like the Bestwood Estate. There was a wood ahead of him, and moonlit fields to the right. The road turned, and Joe passed a fire station.

What was a fire station doing in the middle of no-where? Then he found himself turning left, into a big car park. A large sign said Bestwood Lodge Hotel. Joe drove up to a big, well-lit old building – near enough for him to have some light, but not near enough for him to be seen from inside. He stopped the car.

Joe fumbled around for the internal light switch. Then he went through the glove compartment, finding a pen, a torch, some spare fuses and a packet of screen wipes. He'd no longer got the flashlight, so the torch might come in handy. He scoured the back seat and the compartments on the doors – all he came up with was a bag of boiled sweets. He got out. The night was turning colder. Maybe he should go into the hotel, steal a coat, at least. A coat would cover up his prison clothes and keep him warm. But no, it was too risky. He opened the boot of the car, found a blanket. That was something. There was also a tool kit, which might be handy for doing a break-in. Nothing else.

Some people were coming out of the hotel, their loud voices destroying the calm. Paranoid, Joe got back into the car and sat there, with the interior lights off, wondering what to do. He was only two or three miles from the prison. Maybe he ought to get as far away as possible. But where to? Without Griff to show him the ropes, there was nothing for Joe in London. And, until he did a burglary, he had no money. Not only that, but both the police and the motorway team were after him.

Joe felt very scared and alone. This car park was exactly the sort of place where the police would expect him to go, he decided. Best to leave. A track on the right led into woodland. This must be some sort of country park. He'd hide up there until the time was right for a burglary. He started the car and drove into darkness. The road went on and on, into the woods. After a while, he spotted a turning wide enough to get a car through and backed into it. When he was pretty sure that the car wasn't visible from the road, Joe stopped, turned the lights off and the radio on, then waited.

"I don't think he's coming back," Jan said.

Clare was forced to agree. They were parked outside the squat which Joe Hatton used to share with his mate, Darren, who was still in custody. Hatton had been out for the best part of an hour. If he were going to come to this house, any form of transport would have got him here by now. If he was on foot, he'd never try to get this far.

"We have a report of three white men taking a taxi from Sherwood to the Nottingham Knight Hotel," said the radio. All taxi drivers in the city had been circulated with a request to report such an occurrence, even though the men had probably split up. Clare and Jan looked at each other.

"Responding," Jan said.

The Nottingham Knight was in West Bridgford, a short drive away. With the siren on, they were there in two minutes. So were Ruth and John Farraday, who told them that Joanne Evans was safe and well.

"She described the two men who attacked her," she said.

"And?" Clare asked.

"The descriptions are a possible match for two members of the motorway team, Christopher Stevens and Kevin Hunter."

Clare felt a chill run down her spine.

"You check the pub," Jan told Ruth and John. "We'll cover the car park."

"It's hardly likely to be them," Clare commented, trying not to get excited.

According to the report on the radio, the taxi had been called twenty minutes ago, thirty minutes after the escape. What were the escapers doing hanging about for that long? And, anyway, Clare had seen Gordon Loscoe a half-hour before that – presuming it was Gordon, not just someone who looked like him. All three should be well away by now.

Jan shone her torch around the parked cars. *This is a waste of time*, Clare thought. The three men got away in a four-by-four. Why on earth would they take a taxi to West Bridgford? It made no sense at all.

"Look at this," she told Jan. *This* was an old Rover, in immaculate condition. Or so it appeared, until you went around the other side and saw the smashed window, the wrecked door lock.

"Think they had a go at nicking it?" Jan asked.

"No. There's a *Police Aware* sticker. This was done hours ago."

"Just coincidence then. Let's join the others inside. It's cold out here."

The pub was half full. A couple stood just inside the door playing a pinball machine. You didn't see many of those these days.

"I think Ruth's got something," John said, standing by the busy bar.

The shift's newest member introduced them to the landlord.

"What is this?" the man asked, as he was joined by both Jan and Clare. "Ladies' Night?"

Jan and Clare ignored the comment. Ruth filled them in on what she'd found out.

"There's a Rover outside, been parked there since before dark. One of the customers reported it had been broken into at seven and they've been trying to find the owner since."

"No joy," the landlord said, interrupting. "So I called your lot, like, and they came and put a notice on it. Gave me the name of the owner, too, Chris something."

"That's not all," Ruth said. "About fifteen minutes

ago, three men were observed around the car, trying to get it to start. When a barman went out to see if one of them was the owner, all three got into the car next to it and drove off."

"Got a description?"

"A Peugeot – 309 or 405, he reckoned. A partial plate too."

"What about the men?" Clare asked.

Kelly called the barman over.

"It was dark," he said. "I didn't get a good look. The one who got out of the Rover didn't have a lot of hair, I noticed that. All three were biggish."

"How old?" Clare asked.

"Late thirties, early forties."

Not the escapers, then.

"Was one of them overweight?" Jan.

"Can't say as I noticed."

Clare and Jan looked at each other.

"Did you say you had a name for the owner of the Rover?" she asked the landlord. He got out a scrap of paper.

"Christopher Stevens. Comes from Leamington Spa, according to this. God knows what his car was doing here. Think someone nicked it?"

Until Clare heard the name, that had been the strongest possibility. Now her heart started thumping.

"How long have they been gone?" she asked.

"Ten, fifteen minutes," the landlord said.

"Radio in the description of their car," Clare told

Ruth. "I don't know what they were doing here, but we're definitely on to the motorway team."

7

Nearly half-eleven. The pubs had finished throwing out and there were still police cars all over the shop. Griff kept his head down as he kept moving. He couldn't believe the way the motorway team had betrayed him. In prison, that copper said he'd be looked after. All Griff had to do was con Joe into coming with him. Which he'd done – brilliantly, as far as Griff was concerned. Joe would never have agreed to do a runner, but he wouldn't mess up somebody else's escape, not even if it meant going along himself.

Now Joe was dead and it was Griff's fault. Well, that was tough. *Trust nobody*: that was the first rule of crime. Unfortunately, Griff had failed to observe the rule himself. He'd thought that, with a copper on their side, the motorway team had too much at stake to cheat him. But they knew Griff wouldn't talk because he knew what would happen if he did. All that copper had done was make a few vague promises. Griff thought he was getting a car and a few grand, enough to get him to London and set him up there. Instead, he was on his own. No point in crying about it. In this life, you were always on your own. Best to recognize that and get on with it.

At least he was out. Griff's solicitor said that he was looking at two years, minimum, which would have done his head in. Two *weeks* had been bad enough. No one to talk to but that dumb kid from Mansfield. Nothing but a bit of weak weed to smoke. Now Griff needed to score. He'd walked from Sherwood to Radford, where he had a couple of mates the police didn't know about. One of them was bound to be in.

Or so he thought. The first place was dark and his banging on the door only brought shouts of "Shut that up!" from next door. Dogs began to bark and Griff got on his way. The next place was an ex-girlfriend's. She lived in a flat above a baker's on Ilkeston Road. Griff liked staying with Gina. The smell of freshly baked bread in the mornings always made them wake up hungry, in more ways than one. There was a light on in her living-room window. Griff rang the doorbell below and waited. A sash window half opened. Gina's head appeared through the gap.

"Who's it?"

" 'S'me, Griff."

She was stoned, Griff could tell. He hoped she had some left.

"Thought you were inside."

"Not any more. Let me up, Gina, I want to see you."

"Bad time," Gina said.

A deep voice called from behind her, a string of obscenities telling her to shut the window, it was cold.

"Sorry, Griff, but you wouldn't thank me if I let you in."

"Who is that?" he asked.

"Terence. I'm with Terence now."

Terence was a big black guy, well known on the Green for beating on anyone who rubbed him up the wrong way. He was also a big dealer. Gina always ended up with dealers.

"Throw me down a little rock at least, would you, Gina?"

Behind her, Terence started to swear again.

"Sorry, darlin', he wouldn't like it. Take care now. Bye!"

She closed the window. Griff was about to step back into the street but froze as a police car drove by. It was heading for midnight and he only had a couple of quid in his pocket. There was a taxi firm just along the road, *Checkacab*. He could walk in there, take a taxi to a mate's place in West Bridgford. But he didn't have the money for a taxi. All right, he could do a runner when the taxi pulled up, but that wasn't worth the aggro, not with the police already after him. No, there was only one thing for it. He hoped that Jessica was working tonight.

Ben and Gary were pulling up outside the station when they got a call to say that Maxine Loscoe was home, and willing to talk to them.

"Have you got him yet?" she asked the moment she opened the door, still wearing the fur coat she'd gone out in. Ben couldn't tell whether it was genuine or not.

"Not yet. Can we come in?"

"You'd better."

The house was rented. Ben knew the signs – it was furnished but drab. The carpets and curtains were dirty because no one – landlord or tenant – had any incentive to have them cleaned. There were still cardboard boxes in the hall.

"Has he been?" Ben asked.

"He hasn't," Maxine announced. "And if he does come, I'll kill him!"

"Why?" Gary asked.

"I've just been on to the solicitor. Got him out of bed, I did."

"What about?" Ben.

"The house sale. Eight hundred thousand, we got

for it – enough to pay off all the bills, buy a nice place and have something to live on while Gordon's inside."

"That's nice," Gary told her.

"It would have been. Only thing is, the house is in Gordon's name. Seems contracts have been exchanged without me knowing. How can he do that, in prison?"

"I don't know the legalities," Gary said. "But if the sale's gone through, then surely you've got the money."

"That's just the point," Maxine sobbed, distraught. "Our solicitor said he had it all transferred to a Swiss bank account. Gordon told him that he wanted it there so his creditors couldn't touch it. But now he's gone and I can't touch it either. We're nearly broke! How am I going to pay the rent? What am I going to feed Natalie with?"

"You'll be all right. Come on."

Ben watched as Gary put his arm round Maxine's shoulder and found a tissue for her tears. Ben could never do that. Comforting people was a female officer's job, in his eyes. Ben stepped into the grubby kitchen and radioed Inspector Winter.

"Maxine's home but she hasn't seen hide nor hair of him, sir. It looks like he's done the dirty, sent all their money abroad. Best bet is he's heading for the channel tunnel as we speak."

"All right. See if she's seen anything of Eddie

Broom, would you?"

"The story on Broom is that he's probably abroad too, sir."

"Where do you get that from?"

Ben concocted an explanation. "Natalie Loscoe is going out with Shirley Wilder's son, Curt. It seems that Shirley's left home, gone to the South of France to join Eddie Broom. That could be where Loscoe's heading too."

"See if you can get an address," the Inspector told him.

"I'll look into it," Ben promised, pleased that he'd managed to get the information across without disclosing his relationship with Julie Wilder.

Gary had to know about him and Julie. You couldn't keep stuff like that from your partner. But a relationship with a member of the Wilder family would harm his reputation on the force. And Ben wanted promotion, fast. He was already studying hard for his sergeant's exams.

"If you catch him," Maxine was asking in the living room, "can you make him give the money back?"

"I wouldn't know about that," Gary said.

She stared out of the open curtains on to the shadowy rears of moneyed houses.

"Three years ago, we had nothing," she said. "A tatty council house and a car that hardly went. Then we won the Lottery. I got used to having money.

74

Can you imagine what it'd be like to go back, be poor again, everyone knowing that you'd blown it? I don't think I could stand it. I think I'd do myself in."

"Think of Natalie," Gary said, but Maxine looked unimpressed.

"She's already thrown herself away on that Curt. She'll be pregnant by the time she's sixteen, same as his sister — best part of her life over. If her father was here, he'd…"

She burst into tears again and Gary comforted her, but less demonstratively this time. He and Ben exchanged looks over Maxine Loscoe's shoulder. It was time for them to move on. Which was worse, Ben wondered: never to have anything, or to have everything for a while, but then lose it? He didn't know.

8

Tim Jennings drove out of the city on the A46, towards Leicester, where he had a place. Chris was swearing.

"I loved that car. Now I won't be able to go back for it."

"Call a garage," Kevin suggested, "get them to pick it up, sort it. After all, you're the legal owner."

"That's just the sodding problem," Chris said. "The police are bound to make the connection, keep an eye on it. I can't go near the Rover again."

"But the police haven't actually got anything on us, have they?" Tim felt bound to point out.

"Not until they pick up that Joe kid," Kevin said.

"They won't pick him up," Tim commented. "He'll go to ground."

"Where?" Chris argued. "He hasn't got any-where. So he'll go back to Mansfield, or the Meadows. Probably been caught by now. And he'll blab. He knows we want to kill him, so what has he got to lose?"

Tim had to admit the force of Chris's argument. If Joe testified against them, it meant that the police had them for one burglary. They would never prove the team's other burglaries, or anything to do with that Inspector's murder, but the judge would have a good idea of what they'd got away with, and, presuming they were found guilty, he would give them the longest sentence that the law allowed.

"So what do you reckon?" Tim asked. "Go abroad?"

The police could try to extradite them from France, but would need more proof than they had at the moment.

"Might be safest, yeah."

"Get a move on," Kevin commented, "we could make the same boat as Gordon."

They all laughed. Gordon Loscoe thought that their getting him out was a big favour from his old friend, Eddie. In fact, it had all been a cover for getting Joe Hatton out. And Gordon had paid way over the odds for their services – two grand for the fake passport, twenty grand for expenses in the escape – although this had turned out to be a bargain, given that they'd lost two cars during the evening. Not that they needed the money. Between them, the motorway team had earned far more than Gordon had won on the Lottery, and it was all stashed away in places where neither the law nor the taxman could touch it.

Chris's mobile rang. Only one person outside the team had the number. Tim listened as Chris explained the situation.

"No, we've no idea where he's gone. But he's got Kevin's car. Yeah … I can give you the registration … no, *already*? All right. Get back to me."

He hung up and spoke to the others. "Police have got people waiting at all our places. And they've got a description of this car, with a partial number plate. We're way too conspicuous to be on the road after midnight. Better pull over somewhere."

"There's one of those roadside hotels a little way ahead. We could book in there," Tim suggested.

"Suppose they check the hotels?" Kev.

"We'll be off early," Tim weighed in, "join the rush hour traffic. They're not going to check the place out before then, are they? Anyway, suppose our friend finds Joe for us? We want to be an easy drive away."

"You've got a point," Chris said. "But we'll just take the two rooms – three's a dangerous number tonight. One of us'll have to use the floor."

The motel was coming up on the left. Tim slowed down, hoping that he didn't draw the short straw. He had a bad back, couldn't stand to sleep on the floor. Not that any of them were likely to get much sleep tonight.

"Better call my missis," Kev said, as Chris went to check in. Then he swore.

"What's wrong?" Tim asked him.

"My mobile. I left it in the car."

Gone midnight now. All Joe had to do was start the car and head back to those houses he'd seen earlier. Alternatively, there appeared to be a new estate on the edge of the wood. He could walk over there, do a place, then come back to the car. Even if he set off an alarm, there was no way the police would try and chase someone through a country park at night, especially not the same night as they'd had a prison breakout.

But it was cold and he had no coat. That was the point of doing a burglary – to nick some clothes, get his hands on some ready cash. And then what? Where would he go? Somewhere far from here, that was for sure. What would he do when he got there? Joe had no money, no exam passes, nothing he could do for a job unless you counted burgling. He might manage to sell the car he was in, except that he wouldn't know where to start. Otherwise, he'd have to doss somewhere.

Joe had had enough of sleeping rough when he was hanging out with that plonker, Darren Braithwaite.

At least when you got out of nick the normal way they generally found you a place to live. What did Joe want to do? Go back to Mansfield, he supposed. That was where he knew people.

Unless… All that talk of Griff's about London, the money to be made there, the women, the drugs – he made it sound like the promised land. But you needed contacts, people to trust, or you ended up sleeping in shop doorways at night and selling the *Big Issue* by day. What kind of life was that?

It began to rain. That decided him. He'd try to sleep, do a job early, then drive off in the morning when the rush hour began. Joe pulled the blanket tight around him and closed his eyes.

Almost immediately, a telephone began to ring.

9

Once the rain began, just after twelve, the heart went out of the search. The three men were bound to be well away by now. The road blocks had wasted a lot of manpower with no result whatsoever. Police forces across the country had been alerted about the escape. Photographs of the three were being circulated at all the major ports, airports and the channel tunnel. In Nottingham, there wasn't much left to be done. At twelve-fifteen, Inspector Winter gave the OK for all officers to return to their normal responsibilities.

Clare and Jan got to the station to find Ruth Clarke and John Farraday already there. Ruth made coffee. Her coffee was never good at home, in Clare's opinion, but she managed to make the station instant truly disgusting. Some sugar or a chocolate bar alongside it would make the drink tolerable, but Clare was already having trouble fitting into her uniform. Some people drank when they were depressed. Ruth had been knocking back the gins lately. Clare ate. It seemed like she'd done nothing but eat, sleep and cry since Paul died.

"I'm really sorry about … you know," John Farraday said, sitting down next to Clare. "I didn't know him all that well but he was one of the good guys. He was certainly good to me."

Clare managed half a smile in acknowledgment. She was determined not to burst into tears here, at work.

"If there's anything I can…"

Clare nodded. *If there's anything I can do to help*: these must be the most useless words in the English language. Neil had said something similar in a note to her. If there was anything they could really do – hold your hand, give you a hug, drive you somewhere, talk to you all night when you couldn't get to sleep, then people should say that specific thing. But *anything* meant nothing.

DI Winter plonked a fax on her desk.

"This has just come from CID. All they've got on Brett Griffiths. Some lads from South are staking out his parents' house and the house he shared before we took him in, but this might give us a few ideas – that is, if you still fancy playing detective."

"Thanks," Clare said, without enthusiasm. Brett Griffiths was the one escaper who had no known link to the motorway team. He'd been sharing a cell with Joe Hatton, which was presumably why he'd been in on the escape. Clare couldn't care less about catching Griffiths. He wouldn't lead them to the ones she really wanted, the ones responsible for Paul's death. Still, she began to read.

The phone kept ringing. Eventually Joe found it, in a concealed charger box between the two front seats. He had no intention of answering. The call was either for or from the bloke whose car this was. Either way, Joe was on to a loser.

After a minute, the phone stopped ringing. Joe knew he wouldn't sleep now. At least he had a new toy to play with. He could ring up anyone: his mum, his mates. The police couldn't trace calls made on a mobile, could they? He picked it up, trying to work out which buttons did what. He'd nicked a couple of these in the past, but they all worked differently. There was no dialling tone, which confused him. He typed in the number for "directory enquiries", then pressed a dot, then a different dot. He was about to press the off switch, try again, when a voice spoke to him in the darkness.

"Which town, please?"

"I want a Nottingham number. Name 'Wilder'."

He gave the street name. A computerized voice

read out the number. Joe memorized it, then tapped it in to the small screen. What if Curt didn't answer? What if it was his sister, or his mum? Joe would just hang up.

Joe stared into the dark, at the spooky shadows branching all around him, and shivered. The phone at the other end began to ring.

Their rooms turned out to have a single bed and a double bed. They threw coins for the single, an old system the team used for divvying up unpleasant jobs. First time, they all got heads. Second throw, Chris got heads, while Kev and Tim got tails.

"I hope you two lovebirds will be very happy," Chris joked.

"I'm not sharing a bed with you," Kev announced to Tim. "Your feet smell."

"Floor's all yours then," Tim told him.

"Stop bickering," Chris said. "Phone the kid again."

"What's the point?" Kev asked. "He's probably dumped the car and the phone. He'll be hiding out with some grotty mate of his, trying to think of a place he can run to."

"Maybe," Chris said. "But try it anyway. I'll do the talking if he answers."

"You're the boss," Kev told him. He picked up Tim's phone and pressed *redial*.

It was true, Tim thought. On a job, they were

meant to be equal, but Chris had always been able to lord it over the two of them, always acted *the boss* when it was just the three of them. Not after today, though. Today, they retired.

Kev switched the phone off.

"Why'd you do that?" Chris asked.

"He's there, all right," Kev said. "It's engaged."

Curt was starting to doze off when the phone rang. He wasn't usually in bed this early. Just before she moved abroad, Mum had found a proper school which would take him. It was a double bind – if he got into trouble there, they would insist on seeing his mum. When they found out that she wasn't living at home, they would report it to the social services, who would try to take Curt into care. So for the last few days he'd been playing the system, getting to registration on time, even doing some homework.

He hurried to the phone, not wanting to wake Julie and little Tammy. It would be Nat. His sister had told him that Natalie's father had escaped. Curt was surprised that he could get his fat backside over the prison walls. But the voice at the other end of the phone line wasn't his girlfriend.

"Hey, Curt, how're you doing?"

"Joe?"

Curt used to hang around with Joe when he was living in a squat on the estate. Joe was all right. The older boy treated Curt as an equal, though his mate, Darren, was a complete toss-pot, always throwing his weight around. Joe had tried to get Curt to set him up with Julie, but his sister spotted the invisible "loser" tattoo across his forehead.

"It's me all right," Joe said, with a nervous sounding laugh.

"I thought you were banged up."

"Got out tonight."

"With Gordon Loscoe?"

"'S'right. Has it been on the news?"

"No. He rang up earlier."

"You're kidding? Why?"

"Dunno. I didn't talk to him. What are you doing?"

Joe told him.

"So what do you want with me?" Curt asked.

"I thought you might know of a place to go," Joe said.

"You can't come here," Curt apologized. "My sister's going out with a policeman."

"A *policeman*?"

"Yeah. I know. He's here all the time. That's why—"

"I understand," Joe interrupted, sounding lost, confused.

"What did you break out for?" Curt asked.

"It's a long story. Thing is, these blokes are after me..." He started telling Curt about how he'd nearly been killed two hours earlier. Curt knew about the motorway team – Uncle Eddie was one of them – but Uncle Eddie wouldn't do something like that and anyway, he was in France.

"If they knew you weren't going to tell on them…" Curt began, trying to think of a way for Joe to get out of this mess.

"They don't want to know. They want to kill me."

"You ought to talk to them," Curt said. "What have you got to lose?"

"I need somewhere safe to hide. Where I am is only good until first light."

"Where are you?"

"Bestwood Country Park."

"Never heard of it."

Joe told him where it was. "I'm thinking of doing a job. I need some clothes, money."

"I can lend you a coat and that," Curt offered. "But I don't know if it's safe, you coming here."

"Is he there, the copper?"

"No. He's working. Night shift."

"Will he come there after work?" Joe sounded desperate.

"Doubt it."

"Maybe I'll come then. Trouble is, they're looking for me."

"The police or the motorway team?"

"Both, I reckon. The police don't know what car I'm in, which is something."

"I'll tell you what," Curt said. "Give me your number. I'll sort out a set of clothes and take a look down the street, see how often the police come by. Then I'll call you back. All right?"

"Right," Joe gave him the number and rang off.

Curt went to his meagre wardrobe, wondering what he'd got himself into. He heard Julie moving about in her room, but she didn't appear. His sister would go mad if she knew who he'd been talking to. She might even call her boyfriend. But Curt couldn't let Joe down. It sounded like he didn't have anybody else to turn to.

Joe sat in the car, waiting, worrying. He felt like his nerve was going. He didn't want to pull a job. He could get caught. Some old geezer might clobber him with a stick or shoot him with an unregistered gun. This felt like that kind of area – well off but not rich, a bit wild. There were parts of Mansfield where only a certified nutter would burgle a home because so many uncertified nutters lived in them. It paid to be careful.

The phone rang again. Joe answered it instantly.

"Curt?"

"Joe Hatton?" The voice was deep, immediately recognizable. Joe nearly hung up. "We had a bit of a misunderstanding earlier," the voice continued.

Yeah. You wanted me dead but I didn't, Joe thought, but didn't say.

"Thing is, we wanted to scare you, son, show you we were serious."

"I see." *Keep calm*, Joe told himself. *Don't tell them anything they don't know.*

"It's in our interests to get you somewhere safe. Understand me?"

Safe six feet under, Joe thought. "Not really," he said.

"Get you a good job, new identity, that kind of thing. You don't want to go back inside, now do you?"

"No."

"So what do I have to do to make you trust us again?"

I've never trusted you, Joe thought. *Only tried to keep clear of you.*

"I'll have to think about it," he said. "Give me your number. I'll call you back." That made the caller hesitate. "I'll call *you*," he said, "in twenty minutes. That give you enough time to think?"

"I guess."

"Twenty minutes, then."

He disconnected. Joe found himself shivering. He was out of his depth, and sinking.

Twenty miles away, Chris turned to Tim and Kev. "Do we know anyone called Curt?" he asked.

10

Griff was twenty-two, with minor form for possession and possession with intent to sell. This time he was holding twenty rocks of crack cocaine and was looking at a three- to five-year sentence. Clare studied the murky faxed photograph. In it, he had arrogant eyes and slicked back hair. She felt like she knew his type. Greedy but soft, like Steve, who she used to share a house with. Too soft to stick life in a nick like Nottingham.

Griff hung out at a couple of city centre clubs, but he'd never try his luck there, expecting that the places would be watched. They might have been, if he was the only escaper, but police manpower was fully stretched with three of them out. He was probably miles away from Nottingham by now. Still, there was one place which might be worth a try, a place where he had a personal connection.

"Fancy a ride?" Clare asked Jan.

"Anywhere in particular?"

"The Divers' Club."

"Is that still going?"

"According to this file, it is. Brett Griffiths' sister works behind the bar."

The Divers' Club was at the edge of the city where Radford met Lenton, a short walk from Hyson Green. Despite the logo above the door, which depicted a bikinied swimmer on a diving board, the place wasn't exactly a sporting club. The diving was more of the *ducking and …* type. It was a pick-up joint, haunted by dealers and people sneaking out of their marriages for a quick bit on the side. There were warning notices about drugs all over the place, so the air, typically, was thick with dope smoke. The sight of two female police officers walking in through this haze had no effect on any of the clientele.

"Is Jessica working tonight?" Jan shouted over the bar.

"Why do you want to know?" the barman shouted back.

Clare spotted a girl with long red hair ducking out of the other end of the bar in too much of a hurry.

"Over there," she called to Jan, then went after

her. Jan followed as Clare pushed through sultry dancers, then swung open a door marked *Staff Only*.

"Jessica Griffiths? Jessica, where are you?" They heard someone banging about, but couldn't work out where the sound was coming from. The barman opened the door from the club.

"What's the problem?"

"Is there a back exit from this area?"

"Nah, only door's at the front."

Jan turned to Clare with a grin. "I reckon we've got him!"

The twenty minutes weren't up when the phone rang again. Hesitantly, Joe answered it. This time it was Curt.

"Police are pretty quiet at the moment. I think maybe you could risk coming over."

"All right," Joe said. "I'll come."

"I'd park the car on a different street, if I were you. I'll call you if anything changes."

"OK," Joe said. "But if you need to call, let it ring twice then hang up and immediately call again. That way I'll know it's you."

Joe started the engine and put the car lights on, dimmed. He didn't want to draw attention to himself, but needed to find his way out. As he edged forward, there was a penetrating squeak. A tree was scratching the side of the car. Joe managed to get back on to the track, and hoped that he could remember the way out. The drive had been mostly uphill, so he headed downhill.

Joe was tired. He'd been awake since seven and it was now one. He hadn't eaten for twelve hours and his mouth was dry. He remembered the bag of boiled sweets in the side pocket and reached around for it. A bit of sugar might get his adrenaline going. But he didn't hold the wheel tightly enough and swerved. He slammed the brakes on, narrowly avoiding hitting a tree. He unwrapped a sweet, sucked it, then slowly backed up. A moment later, he almost crashed again. Another car was coming towards him, its lights full on.

The vehicle, a landrover, stopped in front of him. Joe saw the words "Park Ranger" written on the side and panicked. There was just room to manoeuvre around the landrover, so he did, almost hitting the man who was getting out of the vehicle. Joe accelerated downhill, fearful that any moment he would wrap himself around a tree. But his luck was in. He found the car park where he had started out and took a left turn, out towards Bestwood itself.

Had the park ranger had time to take his number? Joe wasn't sure if he'd done anything illegal – except, maybe, breaking park regulations by being there at night. However, there was a fair chance that the ranger would assume the car was stolen (which it was, but Joe doubted that the owner had reported the theft) and inform the police. Joe needed to get a move on. Once he got near to Curt's place, he would dump the car, take his chances on foot with whatever clothes Curt could give him.

Ahead of him, there was an almighty racket. Joe's blood froze. Some kind of new police siren? He braked as he hit the corner and was glad that he had. Charging out from his left-hand side were two huge red fire engines. He was driving past the city's main fire station. For someone, somewhere, this was turning out to be a hot night.

Joe was about to set off again when the phone beside him began to ring. Once. Twice. Three times.

"He's not answering," Chris told the others.

"Never mind," Tim told him. "I've remembered who Curt is."

The back area of the Divers' Club was filthy. Rat droppings littered the stairs to the cellar. Jan flicked on the lights and went down. Clare searched upstairs. The kitchen looked like it had been designed as a breeding ground for cockroaches.

"Jessica?" she yelled again.

A toilet flushed. The girl with the long red hair came out of a cubicle at the far end of the area.

"Jessica Griffiths?" Clare asked.

"Yeah. What do you want me for?" She sounded defensive, possibly guilty.

"Why did you run in here?"

"I was desperate to go, all right? What d'you want?"

"It's about your brother, Brett."

Jessica tilted her eyes towards the crumbling ceiling. Clare thought she heard movement nearby. Maybe it was only the cistern refilling.

"What's he done now?" Jessica asked.

"Escaped from prison," Jan told her.

Jessica laughed. "Him? Escaped? Pull the other one! How'd he do it – float out on a cloud of dope smoke?"

"We thought you might know where he is," Clare told her.

"We're not exactly a close family," Jessica said. "I heard he was in the nick but I haven't been to visit him or anything. So I haven't a clue where he might have gone. Mind if I go back to the bar? I'll be missed."

"Just hang around for a couple of minutes," Clare said, certain that the girl was hiding something. "Don't worry, I'll square it with your boss."

Jan continued to check out the cellar. Clare opened cupboards and inspected the filthy toilet. There was no window to escape through, nowhere for Griff to have gone unless he was in the club when they'd arrived and they'd somehow failed to spot him. In which case, it would be too late and Griff would be long gone. Jan reappeared.

"Nothing. You?"

Clare shook her head.

"If he shows up," Jan told Jessica, "call us. He won't last long on the out. His best bet is to give himself up and do his time."

"I couldn't agree with you more," Jessica said. "But he won't show up here. He always told me it was beneath me, working in a dump like this. Like he's done better for himself, seeing as where he ended up."

They listened for a moment after she'd gone, but there was no sound.

"I could have sworn I heard something," Clare said, as they were leaving.

The fire engines were actually a stroke of luck. Who would notice the dark-coloured car following in their wake? Thanks to them, Joe got into town quickly, even jumping a couple of lights. Going through the city centre was the only hairy bit. He clocked two police pandas, but neither of them was near enough to see his face. There was another one on London Road, but it didn't follow Joe when he turned right into the Meadows, then abandoned the car on the edge of the Maynard Estate.

He took the mobile phone with him, and the car keys, just in case. He even put the car alarm on. The night was cold and dark, with little moonlight between the clouds. At least it had stopped raining.

On Curt's road, Joe gave the lightest of taps on the door. It opened immediately. His friend let him inside.

"Got to be quiet," Curt said. "My sister and the baby are upstairs."

"What about your mum?" Joe asked.

"She's away. You can go in her room if you need a bit of kip. Let me show you the clothes first."

"I'm starving," Joe told him. "Got anything to eat?"

"Bread and marge. Peanut butter. That's about it."

"Sounds great. You're a mate, Curt."

He wolfed a sandwich down, then went upstairs. The clothes which Curt could afford to give him were a bit basic – T-shirt, manky sweater and worn-out jeans – but at least the two youths were the same size.

"You're a star," Joe said.

"There's a big parka in the wardrobe that Eddie left behind. You can have that, too. You'll need it, this weather."

"Are you sure?"

"It doesn't suit me," Curt said, with a smirk. "Won't suit you, either, but it'll keep you warm. What are you gonna do?"

"Dunno," Joe said, as a wave of tiredness came over him. "I need a bit of kip. Are you sure it's all right if…"

"Should be. Tammy usually wakes up around six, though. You ought to be gone by then."

"All right. Have you got an—"

"Alarm clock? Yeah. I'll set mine for half-five, come and wake you."

"Thanks, Curt, you're brilliant. I'll pay you back somehow, sometime."

"Yeah, sure. Get some kip."

Joe remembered to turn off the mobile phone before he got into bed. At least, it looked like it was turned off. Its time display said 1:36 a.m. With luck, he would get four hours' sleep, enough to keep him going. He closed his eyes and was out like a light.

Jessica came back for Griff when the club was closing down, at two.

"You can get out now," she called up to where he was squashed.

"Sure they're not outside?"

"Positive, I just looked."

Griff was hiding in the chute which was used to pump in beer deliveries. It was cold, damp and cramped and he was desperate for a smoke. Both his arms and legs had gone to sleep. But at least he was safe. If the policewoman who'd searched the cellar before had opened the chute and shone her torch up it, she'd have seen him. But she'd missed the thing altogether. Now Jessica opened it to let Griff out.

"Can't move," he said. "I'm stuck."

"I'll give you a hand," she told him, reaching in. She grabbed his foot and yanked it. Griff managed to push against the wet wall.

"Got you!" Jess said.

Then he was sliding down and his sister couldn't get out of the way quickly enough. Griff tried to twist around her but his legs were still all cramped up and there were beer barrels to the side. He crashed into one of them, ending up in a heap on the stone floor with Jessica beside him. He groaned.

"What's wrong?" Jess said. "I'm the one who got knocked over."

"I'll tell you what's wrong," Griff said, trying to get up and failing. "I've broken my leg!"

11

The message came on the radio at two-fifteen, as Jan and Clare completed a circuit of the Meadows area.

"Be on the lookout for a brown Mondeo, last three licence plate numbers VSG, seen in Bestwood Country Park in the last half-hour. Suspicion of taking without the owner's consent, dangerous driving and possible use in the commission of a theft."

"Brown Mondeo, did they say?" Jan asked, pulling up on the edge of the Maynard Estate and pointing at a car parked underneath a broken street-lamp. "Are those the right licence plates?"

Clare could just read them. The last three letters were USG. "Near enough," she said.

The car didn't look like it had been abandoned.

She got out and had a look. A red flicker inside the vehicle showed that the alarm had been activated. The car was muddy around the sills. Clare walked around it and found a big scratch along both passenger side doors. It looked fresh.

"He might be coming back," Clare said, getting back into the police panda. She told Jan about the alarm. "The licence-plate matching could be a coincidence."

"Better check if it's been stolen."

"Good point." Clare radioed the details in, giving the full licence-plate number. The details came back within a minute.

"Car belongs to a Kevin Hunter of Birmingham. It's not been reported stolen."

"Kevin Hunter," Clare repeated, excitedly. "He's the driver for the motorway team!"

Jan radioed Oxclose Lane. The voice she got on the other end was Phil Church, CID's liaison with the Solihull Task Force investigating the motorway team.

"Park a discreet distance away, but don't let the Mondeo out of your sight," he said. "If Hunter's in Nottingham, there has to be a connection with Joe Hatton's escape."

"Hold it!"

Tim braked.

"I don't believe this," Kevin said. "That's my car."

"Keep going," Chris said.

"I want it back!"

"Got a spare set of keys on you?" Chris.

"No."

"Well, we need to find Hatton first then, don't we? Shirley's place is just round the corner."

They parked at the end of the street. As they did, Chris's phone rang. He hardly spoke, grunting, "right" and "we've seen it, yeah." Finally, he said, "We're outside now. OK. Later," and hung up.

"That was our friend," he told the others. "Police have already noticed your car, Kev, and they've put a watch on it. We nearly blew it there."

"Think they're watching the Wilder house, too?" Kev asked.

"Not at the moment. But we'd better make ourselves scarce for a while, come back for the boy a bit later."

Tim drove out towards the river. "What if the police work out that he's at the Wilder house?" he asked.

"They haven't made that link yet. No reason for them to."

"But the house is connected to us," Kev pointed out.

"Only because of Eddie," Chris said. "And Old Bill know that Eddie's abroad."

None of the team believed it when Eddie announced that he was moving to France, taking

Shirley Wilder with him. Blokes of his means could have much better quality crumpet than a thirty-something slapper like Shirley. But Eddie wanted Shirley and he wanted to get out. As soon as the loose end represented by Joe Hatton was cut off, the other three would go, too. Tim could hardly wait. He drove around the dark embankment, found a quiet spot, and parked. If Joe managed to get to the car, made a run for it, he was bound to come this way.

"I still don't get it," Kev said. "Why is this Hatton kid at Shirley's place?"

"He's a mate of the boy, in't he?" Tim suggested. "Curt."

"Or he's knocking off the sister," Chris suggested. "Julie. She's a looker, according to Eddie. Said he'd be tempted himself if he weren't practically her uncle."

"I expect that's it," Kev said. "So how are we going to handle her? We don't want to upset Eddie, do we?"

"Sod Eddie," Chris said. "It'll be worse for us if that kid gets out of there alive."

"If he's in there," Tim said.

"He's not got anywhere else to go," Chris told them. "He's in there all right."

Tim felt a chill. There'd been enough killing already. He didn't want to go and shoot up Eddie's girlfriend's house.

"I say we give him a bell," he suggested, "try and make a deal with him."

"A deal!" Chris mocked. "After I tried to shoot him?"

"Got to be worth a try," Tim said, in his most persuasive voice. "Anyway, it's not safe to go in at the moment. And the Wilder kids might talk some sense into Joe. You don't rat to the police. That's the first rule."

"Bollocks!" Chris said. "People do what they have to do to survive. *That's* the first rule."

"We could at least try," Tim suggested.

"He's right," Kev said. "Go in with guns and it could get messy."

Chris looked cornered, angry. "OK," he said. "Let's think about this."

12

Night shifts are no longer than other shifts. They just feel longer. You can do them for years and years, but your body still has trouble adapting. Food, in particular, is a problem. Doesn't matter how much or how little you eat, it never feels right, and the appetite can strike at the strangest times. It was two forty-five in the morning. Clare had been watching a parked car for half an hour. They'd been on the way back to the station for a meal break when they spotted the car. Now, her stomach gurgled.

"Was that you, or me?" Jan asked.

"Me."

"I've got a Twix you can have if you're desperate."

"No, thanks. I've eaten enough chocolate lately."

Clare had a couple of rolls in the fridge at the station. Tuna and low calorie mayonnaise on whole-wheat bread. But the way things were going, she might not get back to the station until the end of the shift. When you were on nights, junk food ruled.

Surveillance was boring work. The last time Clare had done any, it had been with Paul, trying to nail the motorway team. She tried not to think about that now.

"How's your mum?" Jan asked.

"All right. She's been brilliant to me, these last two weeks."

"You've been living there?"

"Mostly. Sam and Ruth try their best to help, but Ruth's miserable herself and Sam finds it hard to talk about death. Gary's great, but he's out a lot with Umberto…"

"There are times when a girl needs her mum," Jan said. "But it'd be a backward step to move in with her, wouldn't it?"

"I guess," Clare said, uncomfortable because Jan was one jump ahead of her. "I'm not sure about anything any more. Right now, I don't even know whether I want to stay in the job."

Jan was silent for a while. Clare nearly said something like *Don't mention that to anyone*, but Jan was her mentor. Her discretion went without saying.

"What would you do?" Jan asked. "Go back to university?"

"To be an architect?" Clare laughed. "That seems so long ago. I feel a million years older. I don't know what I'd do if I left the job. What would you do?"

Jan opened her bar of Twix and, without comment, passed half of it to Clare, who gobbled it down gratefully. "Kevin's after me to have another baby," she said. "Of course we'd have to find time to have sex first. He'd be happy if I gave up the force. He'll be a consultant in three or four years, provided things go according to plan. Me, I'd like to be an inspector, eventually. I might manage that if I have another baby, but it's doubtful."

"I asked what you'd do if you left the force," Clare reminded her.

"I can't imagine leaving the job," Jan said. "Not ever, I'm here until retirement or until they carry me off in a wooden box." She realized what she'd said. "Oh, hell, Clare! I'm sorry."

"It's all right," Clare said. "I have to get used to it."

It was true. She had to. Clare was used to her brother's death now, and didn't get upset when someone mentioned Angelo, or when there was a car accident on TV, or when she saw a kid who looked like him in the street. But she didn't deliberately talk about him, either. If she met someone new, she said that she was an only child, not that her brother had been killed in a hit-and-run accident.

This was better than dealing with the embarrassed sympathy of a stranger. Now she had another death to get used to.

How long would it take her to get over Paul? Clare knew that she hadn't even begun. Rationally, she knew that her lover was dead, but emotionally, she hadn't begun. With Angelo, Clare didn't start to accept what had happened until she found the person responsible for his death. But Paul Grace was probably shot by a professional killer. Men like that were hardly ever caught.

The car was cold. You needed the engine on to run the heater and they didn't want to draw attention to themselves any more than they were doing just by being there.

"Think we could ask someone to drop us off some coffee?" Clare asked.

"Don't see why not. I'm the sarge, after all. Alternatively, we could get John and Ruth to take over."

"Not Ben and Gary?"

"No. Ben's got urgent paperwork to do for tomorrow morning."

"Let's stay here a while longer," Clare said. If one of the motorway team was going to return to this car, she wanted to find out what he was up to.

"All right," Jan said. "I'll get on the radio, ask someone to drop off some coffee."

"And see if they can bring some food over," Clare said. "I'm starving."

*   *   *

Tammy started crying at twenty to three. She'd been snuffly for a couple of days and Julie was worried about her catching something serious. The house got colder every day. They couldn't afford to have the heating on as much as Julie would like. Mum had paid all the bills before she left and she'd promised to send more money later. Even so, money was tight.

Julie was tempted to fiddle the social. It was easily done – get someone to sign on in Mum's place and Julie could get Mum's supplementary benefit as well as Curt's child allowance. Only problem was, if Ben found out, he'd go ballistic. Her boyfriend had said as long as Julie was law-abiding, he didn't care about the rest of her family. But the law was mean and heartless. It was sometimes hard to be honest when you were poor.

Julie wiped Tammy's nose and gave her a cuddle. She'd be all right, Julie was pretty sure, but it was easy to get paranoid sometimes, especially when your mother wasn't around to give advice. She was about to get back into bed when the telephone rang. Phone calls at this time meant trouble. Shivering, she went downstairs and answered it.

The voice at the other end was unfamiliar.

"Julie, love, sorry to bother you."

"Who is this?"

"It's Chris. I'm a mate of Eddie's."

"So? It's nearly three o'clock in the morning."

"I know, love, but, thing is, I need to speak to Joe and he's turned his mobile off."

"Joe? Who's Joe?"

"Lad who's staying with you. Is he up?"

"Not only is he not 'up', he's not here. And I don't know who you are, so *good night*."

She put the phone down and immediately began to worry. Chris… Had Uncle Eddie mentioned a "Chris". Suppose he had a message for her? Something about Mum. But he'd have said, wouldn't he? Instead, he'd gone on about a Joe. The only Joe who Julie knew was a lad who'd asked her out once. He used to hang around with Curt. At least, he did until he went inside.

Inside. According to the local news, two other men had escaped with Gordon Loscoe tonight. Suppose this Joe was one of them? Why would he come here? But Joe had come before, Julie remembered, late at night, looking for Curt. She'd had Ben with her at the time, and sent him away. The boy had been arrested the next day, the same day that Ben's inspector had been shot.

Julie took the phone off the hook and went back to bed, but it was no use. She couldn't sleep. There was too much on her mind, not least this Joe business. He wasn't here, was he? There was a quick way to find out. She got up, put on a dressing gown, and went to her mother's room. Actually, Julie had thought about making this room her bedroom, as it was slightly bigger than hers, and had a decent double bed. Only trouble was, the one night she'd tried it, Tammy wouldn't get off until four in the morning.

Quietly, Julie opened the door. The room was dark, because the curtains were closed, which was unusual in itself. *Why am I tiptoeing around?* Julie asked herself. *This is my house.* She switched on the light.

"Get away from me!" A naked youth jumped out from beneath the duvet and grabbed the bedside light as a weapon. Julie stood her ground, looking at him calmly until he recognized her, put down the lamp and lifted the duvet to cover up his manhood.

"What the hell are you doing here?" she asked.

"She's taken the phone off the hook," Chris told the others. They were still parked on the embankment, a two-minute drive from the Wilder house.

"You think she was telling the truth?" Tim asked.

"Why should she? She doesn't know who I am," Chris told them.

"So what do we do now?" Kev.

"Depends. Think the police are going to stay on the Mondeo all night?"

"Looks like it," Kev again.

"You're going to have to forget the car, then. We'll just go into the Wilder house, take out the kid and get on our way."

"You think we'll make it to the coast, do you?" Tim asked.

"They haven't got the number of this car, have they?"

They hadn't, because Tim had had the foresight to register it in his girlfriend's name at her address.

"If we're going to get out of the country, I need to call Cheryl," he said.

He'd lived with Cheryl for two years, a fact that he'd managed to conceal from the police when they arrested him for the raid on the footballer's house. That was a trick he'd learnt from Eddie: don't have an official address, and, if you do, never use it as your home. As far as the police knew, Tim lived with his divorced mother in Leicester.

"Call later, when we know what's going on," Chris said.

"I'm not happy," Tim said. "Three of us in one car – the shooting'll get reported, linked to the escape. The police will know exactly who we are. It's messy. We'll never make it to the coast."

"You got a better plan?" Chris asked.

"Leave it another couple of minutes, then phone the mobile again," Tim suggested. "If he's there, Julie will have woken him up by now. Talk some sense into him. Maybe use the girl as a go-between."

"We can do that better in the house with a gun to his head," Chris said.

"Maybe. But there's a squad car just round the

corner. The minute they hear gunshots, what chance do you give us of getting away?"

"Why can't *you* take the coffee?" Ruth asked Gary at twenty to three. "After all, it's Ben's case tomorrow, not yours."

Gary shrugged, not wanting to rock the boat. He and Ben had given up searching for escaped prisoners and returned to their paperwork. Or, to be more precise, Ben's paperwork. He was busy typing and Ruth was pointedly ignoring him. An awkward atmosphere prevailed. Gary was avoiding the awkwardness by watching Channel 4 on the tiny black and white telly they kept in the corner of the parade room. It didn't matter that the telly was black and white because they were showing a 1930s screwball comedy with Irene Dunne. Gary loved this kind of movie. Having the telly on was one of the few perks of doing a night shift.

"Gary?" Ruth repeated.

"Exercise'll do you good," he said.

She held up a sandwich box. "Are these Clare's?"

Gary nodded. "Where exactly are they, anyway?" he asked.

"On the Maynard Estate," Ruth said. "According to Jan, they're just round the corner from that Lottery girl – what's her name? – Julie Wilder."

At the mention of Julie, Ben looked up. "Who's parked round the corner from the Wilders'?"

"A car belonging to one of the motorway team," Ruth answered, in a neutral voice. "Jan and Clare are watching it."

"And has anybody been round to see Julie and Curt?"

"I don't think so. The Wilders have nothing to do with it. Car's probably been dumped there, that's all."

She and John left. "We'll take a run around after," John said. "Back in half an hour, if everything's clear."

"She's going to find out sooner or later," Gary told Ben, when Ruth was out of earshot. "So's the Inspector."

"I don't see why," Ben said. "It's just a casual thing. Anyway, Julie's not a criminal."

"But she's connected."

"Now that Shirley and Eddie have left the country, surely…"

Gary shook his head. "Curt's still there, and Eddie might come back."

Ben turned away from the typewriter. "Maybe I should have gone."

Gary didn't understand. "What's the problem?"

"I don't know," Ben said. "Suppose they're using her house to hide up in?"

"And why would they do that? Look, Ben, if they are there, you don't really want to know about it, do you? It'd mean that your Julie's helping them. But they're probably miles away, following Eddie Broom out of the country, taking Joe Hatton with them."

"If Joe Hatton's with them," Ben said, "he's not alive."

13

"Who let you in here?" Julie asked the naked youth.

"Curt."

"That's aiding and abetting an escape. You want him stuck in Glen Parva because of you, do you?"

"No, I ... I don't have anywhere else to go."

"Well, you can't stay here. Why did you escape if you don't have anywhere to go?"

"It's a long story. Do you mind if I put some clothes on?"

"All right," Julie said.

He hesitated. "If you think I'm turning my back on you," Julie said, "you can forget it. I don't want to get hit."

"I wouldn't do that."

"I'm not going to give you the chance."

She watched as he put on some old clothes of Curt's.

"Those won't get you far. Has he given you a coat?"

"He said there was a parka in the wardrobe." Julie got it out. Eddie was no taller than Joe, but he was much stockier, and it looked silly.

"Have you got someone to share this with?" she asked, mockingly.

The boy sat on the bed, looking crumpled, exhausted. It was getting on for three in the morning, and he looked out of it. Julie, however, had learnt to get by on snatches of sleep.

"Tell me everything that's happened," she said.

He told her.

Ben finished typing the report. Gary was watching some old movie with a sexy white woman in silk pyjamas, and chuckling a lot. Ben would never understand his partner's sense of humour. He thought about Julie, and the motorway team. Julie's problem was her background. Her mother had married a petty criminal and ended up as the mistress of a major one: Eddie Broom, the reconnaissance man for the motorway team. Fears ran through Ben's head. Suppose Eddie had run off with the rest of the team's money? They could be threatening Julie and Curt as a way of pressuring Eddie to give it back.

It wouldn't hurt to call her. Julie always said that if he needed to talk to her Ben could call any time, day or night. There was risk involved. The conversation could be traced from either end. Better, perhaps, to walk down the road, use a phone box. But it would still be easy for an investigator to work out who had made the call. Ben decided to log his action, just in case something happened later on. If challenged, he would come clean about going out with Julie. It wasn't against the law, after all.

He wrote down in his notebook: *3.05 a.m. Rang Julie Wilder*. He dialled the number, then added the note: *Line engaged*.

Who the hell was she talking to?

"They know you're here," Julie told Joe.

"How?"

"Someone called Chris rang ten, fifteen minutes ago."

Joe swore. He was almost calm now. Julie had woken him from a bad dream, where he was waiting in the shed with the others, like earlier today. Then, instead of the JCB arriving, Chris had walked through the door, with a gun. He shot them all, again and again and again. It was a relief to be woken up.

Joe had always fancied Curt's sister. Now she stood before him, an accusing angel.

"How do they know you're here?" Julie asked.

"What the hell do you think you're playing at, letting them know a thing like that?"

Joe thought back. He had answered the phone "Curt" when it turned out to be Chris. But how would they know which Curt it was? Haltingly, he explained this to Julie.

"You idiot," she said. "They'll be round here now. You've got to get away."

"They're probably outside, watching," Joe protested.

"In that case," Julie said, "why haven't they come in to get you? They can't be sure."

"Is there a back way out?"

Julie shook her head. "Why don't you ring them up – you might be able to find out something, stall them at least."

"I don't have the number," Joe said, then remembered that the mobile phone was switched off. He got it out and turned it on again.

"How do I know if I can trust them?" he asked Julie.

"You can't," she said. "The only people you can trust are the police."

Joe laughed. "They kept offering me deals. Testify against the motorway team and they'd let me straight out after the trial. Sure, and get killed."

"But the team tried to kill you anyway."

"Whose side are you on?" Joe asked. "My head's spinning here."

Julie stood at the window, parting the curtains so that she could look down the street.

"I'm not on anybody's side," she said. "I don't want to get into trouble and I do want you out of this house. I'm in a complicated enough situation as it is."

"How do you mean?"

"My boyfriend's a policeman, if you must know, and my mum's going out with a member of the motorway team. Funny, eh?"

"It's too complicated for me," Joe admitted. He didn't know what to do.

"Why did you come here?" Julie asked.

"To get some clothes and grub."

"Then I think it's time you moved on."

The mobile phone on the bed began to ring.

"Stall them," Julie said. "See what they want, then tell them to call you back." Joe did as she said.

"Where are you?" Chris asked, his voice teetering on fury.

"I stopped," Joe told him, "had a kip."

"Where?"

"I think it's called B–Bestwood Park," Joe stuttered.

"You're lying. So, listen, we need to make a deal."

"What kind of deal?" Joe asked, tentatively.

"You can come out of the country with us. We've got a plane. You'll get enough money to set you up for life."

"If you're leaving the country," Joe said, "why do you care about me? It doesn't matter if I testify against you or not."

"They have these things called extradition treaties," Chris said.

"How much money?" Joe asked. He had to sound serious.

"A hundred grand."

"That's a lot."

"It's your lucky day, son." Chris tried to sound humorous, failed.

"And what guarantees do I have?"

"I guess you just have to trust us."

"All right," Joe said. "Let me think about it. Give me your number."

"No way."

"You said *trust*, right? Give me your number. I'll call you back in twenty mins." Reluctantly, Chris gave him the number. Julie hurried for a pen.

"Is someone there with you?" Chris asked. "You're not in the car."

"I am in the car," Joe lied.

"In that case, you'll find a pen in the left side pocket. See, there's one with a torch on the end of it."

Joe remembered the pen, but hadn't noticed the light on the end. It must have been under the cap.

"Got it," he said, as Julie handed him pen and paper. "All right. I'll call you back." He hung up.

"Do you trust them?" Julie asked, helping him on with the parka.

"Not in a million years. But if I can figure a way to get the money off them, it might be worth the risk."

"And if you can't?"

Joe shrugged. "They had a copper killed, didn't they? I wouldn't mind if they all went inside. Think the police would get me a wotsit, a new identity?"

"They might," Julie said. "I could call them for you now, ask."

"I dunno," Joe said. "Ratting on blokes like that … thanks, though. Thanks for not turning me in."

She saw him to the door. "Good luck," she said, and kissed him on the cheek.

The kiss kept Joe going for the short walk from her house to his stolen car.

"He wasn't in the car," Chris said.

"How do you know?" Tim asked.

"I made up this story about there being a pen with a torch on the end and he acted like he'd found it."

"Idiot. So where is he?"

"I reckon he's at the Wilders'."

"Then let's go there," Tim said, starting the engine. He was fed up of waiting here, doing nothing. He could be asleep in his bed at the warm motel.

"Take the long way round," Chris said. "I don't want to go past that cop car."

Clare finished her tuna roll and realized that she needed the loo. She shouldn't have had that coffee.

"Is there anywhere I can…?"

"Ssssh!" Jan said. "I think someone's coming. Rear-view mirror."

It was a shadow, that was all, but a moving shadow. It reached the brown Mondeo and stopped. They could see him now, a big figure in some kind of heavy coat, with a hood over his head. Clare heard the *pfffft!* which meant that the car alarm had been deactivated.

"Let him get inside," Jan reminded Clare, "then you go and cop him while I block the road. Ready? Steady. *Go!*"

Clare jumped out of the car and ran across the road. The figure in the car glanced round, but she couldn't see his face. He was looking over her shoulder at the police car accelerating towards him.

"Get out of the car!" Clare yelled. "Now!"

As she reached him, he swung the driver's door at her, hard, so that it caught her full in the stomach, knocking the wind out of her. She stumbled backwards and fell to the ground. *You stupid girl!* Clare told herself as he got out of the car. The youth stepped on her, all of his weight on her left ankle. Then he ran off in the direction he'd come from.

Clare couldn't feel her left foot. She heard the sound of footsteps – not heavy, so it couldn't be a big man after all – and the sound of Jan reversing the car, going after him. *Don't run over me*, she begged silently, as the Panda swerved around her.

Two minutes later, Jan was back.

"This place is like a maze," she said. "Half the streets are blocked off to stop joyriders. I didn't have a chance. Hey, are you all right?"

Clare found herself crying. "I think he broke my ankle," she said.

14

"If we stay here much longer," Tim warned from the driver's seat, "the police are bound to notice us."

They'd only been parked five minutes, but a patrol car had been down the road twice already. Luckily, they were in an unlit corner and had plenty of time to duck.

"Heads down!" Kev hissed.

A burly figure in a parka ran straight past without noticing the car or its occupants.

"Who's that?" Kev asked.

"How the hell should I know?" Chris said.

"He's at the Wilder house," Tim said, looking through the rear view mirror, "knocking on the door."

"Didn't Eddie used to have a coat like that?" Kev.

Tim remembered. It was one of Eddie's *surveillance coats*. Anyone seeing him in it would remember the coat, not the person inside it. That was the theory behind the coat.

"Door's opening," Kev said.

"Who is it?" Tim asked. He half expected Eddie to be there, all that stuff about disappearing abroad to be a fairy tale.

"It's the girl. She doesn't seem sure whether to let him in or not. Think it's the kid?"

"There's a quick way to find out," Chris said. He was dialling. Tim turned round as the phone at the other end began to ring. He was just in time to see the boy in the parka jump like he'd been shot. It was him all right. The girl let him in.

"Why did you have to come back here?" Julie asked Joe as she let him in, a walking phone box.

"I didn't have anywhere else to go."

"You say the police were watching the car?"

"One of them nearly got me."

The mobile phone's ring seemed louder and louder. Julie sat on the stairs, head in her hands. The other phone was still off the hook. What to do? All she really wanted was to get rid of Joe. She wanted to ring Ben, tell him to come and take the boy away. A fiasco like this was all they needed to split the two of them up.

"You have to go," she told him.

"They're looking for me."

Still the phone rang, an insistent, awful *bleep bleep*.

"Then you have to give yourself up. Testify against them. They're murderers. They deserve to be put away."

"They're not killers, they're burglars. They couldn't be killers. They were inside when the cop got shot."

"But they tried to shoot you, didn't they?" Julie pleaded, as the phone's ring seemed to grow uglier, more insistent. "You don't owe them anything."

"Maybe they didn't mean to kill me. Maybe they just wanted to give me a scare, like they said."

"You *idiot*!" Now Julie was shouting. "Can't you see that you'll be dead before daylight if you don't give yourself up to the police! Do it! Do it now!"

"What's going on?" Curt asked, stumbling down the stairs in only a T-shirt and underpants. He reached for the phone, which Julie had taken off the hook, then realized that it wasn't the one ringing and put it back in its cradle.

"Aren't you going to answer that phone?" he asked.

"Why did you let him in here?" Julie yelled at her brother. "Didn't I tell you you had to stay out of trouble or you'll end up in care?"

"He had nowhere else to go," Curt said.

Joe stood by the door. The phone, still ringing, was in his hand.

"I'll go if you want," he said. "I'll take my chances."

"Turn yourself in," Julie said.

"He can't do that," Curt protested. "Eddie's mates'd end up in the nick. Eddie too, probably, in the end. They're bound to snitch on him if they get caught. And where would that leave Mum? Have a heart, Julie. Let him stay until we've sorted something out."

Outside, there was a police siren. Julie flinched. The phone kept ringing. It felt like the whole street must be able to hear it. Upstairs, Tammy began to bawl. Now the other phone began to ring. Julie felt like she was going mad.

"Answer that bloody phone!" Curt shouted.

"Get off the phone!" Ben hissed at the receiver. It was 3:20. Who was Julie talking to? Maybe it was Curt, having a middle of the night conversation with his girlfriend, Natalie, about her runaway father. Yes. That would be it. No need to panic. He dialled again and this time the phone rang, but nobody answered. Gary tapped him on the shoulder.

"Come on. We're out in the car. Maynard Estate."

"What's happened?"

"Jan's had to take Clare to hospital. There's someone running round in a dark-coloured parka. Might be a member of the motorway team."

"And what are they doing on the Maynard Estate?" Ben asked.

Gary shrugged. "Your guess is as good as mine."

Reluctantly, Ben put the phone down. Whatever was happening, he guessed that it had something to do with the Wilders. There were plenty of other criminal families on the estate, but none that was connected with the motorway team, as far as he knew.

"I think we'd better go to Julie's," he said, following Gary to the car.

"Can't," Gary said. "Boss wants us to mind this brown Mondeo."

When they got there, it didn't look to Ben like there was any point in minding the Mondeo. A door hung open. The keys were in the ignition. Whoever had abandoned it would expect the car to be nicked within the hour. This was the Maynard Estate, after all.

"I'm going round to Julie's," Ben said. "I'll be back in ten minutes. You can handle this till then. Nothing's going to happen. Take my word for it."

"You're in charge," Gary said, with a slight edge to his voice.

As Ben got out of the car there was a radio report. Ruth and John had seen nothing.

"*The man in the parka isn't on the move,*" John said. "*He's probably hiding on the embankment. We're going to…*"

Ben didn't hear the rest. He walked rapidly to Julie's street.

"Took your time, didn't you?" Chris said, when Joe answered the phone.

Joe tried to remain calm. "You weren't meant to call me, I was meant to call you," he said. "You should have waited. I have things to work out."

"What things?"

"Plans," Joe said, improvising.

"We know where you are, Sunny Jim." The man's voice was menacing now. "You can't get away."

"And you can't get in here. The whole area is crawling with police."

As Joe spoke, there was another siren. It was only a matter of time before the police came upon the motorway team, took them in. Or so he hoped.

"A hundred grand," Chris repeated. "In your hand. Today."

"Where?" Joe asked.

"Abroad. Safe."

"I don't speak any languages," Joe told him.

Chris did his sarcastic laugh and it suddenly all became too much for Joe. He burst into tears, letting the phone drop on to the settee. Julie picked it up.

"This is Julie Wilder," she said.

"Got you doing his talking for him now, has he?" Joe could still hear Chris speak, his words muffled but manic.

"He's scared," Julie replied.

"He ought to be."

"You've got to give him a way to trust you."

"You tell him to, love."

"I'm not your love."

"Do it for Eddie, then. You know he'd want you to."

"Yes. I do know."

Julie moved away from Joe, so he couldn't hear the voice at the other end of the line. Was she about to sell him out?

"I'll tell you what," she said. "Get Eddie to ring me. If Eddie tells me that Joe'll be safe, I'll tell Joe to trust you."

A pause while Chris replied.

"I don't believe you," Julie said. "You … what?"

She switched the phone off and whispered to Joe. "There's a policeman about to knock on the door. You've got a choice. Now's the time to give yourself up, if you're going to. Or hide!"

15

"Is it broken?" Clare asked, as the doctor in Casualty examined her rapidly swelling ankle at half-past three in the morning.

"You won't be playing tennis for a while," the doctor said, "or doing any running of any kind. But no, not broken. You've either badly strained the ligament in your left ankle, or it could be torn. We won't know for sure until the swelling goes down. Whoever stood on you may have chipped the little bit of bone which connects the ligament to the ankle bone. If that's happened, we'll have to put the ankle in plaster for several weeks. But you'll live."

"How long will I have to be off work?"

The doctor shrugged. "A month, at least. I'm going to get you some crutches, which you should use until the weekend. Please return them. You'd be surprised how many people don't. And you need to take these three times a day, with meals."

He handed her a jar of red tablets. Clare thanked him.

"You're welcome. You'll excuse my lack of bedside manner, but you jumped the queue and I have another eleven patients to see. I suggest you make an appointment to see your own doctor in two days' time. He'll tell you if you need an X-ray. Goodnight."

"Could be worse," Jan said, but Clare was feeling sorry for herself.

"He didn't even ask if I could get home all right," Clare said. "I thought they'd at least give me a bed for the night. I'm in agony."

"Is it just your ankle?" Jan asked, matter of factly.

Clare seemed to realize that she was whining, and calmed down. "Just the ankle, yeah."

"Come on then. I'll help you to the car." Jan led Clare through the waiting area.

"You were lucky they could see you so fast," she said. "Most people have to wait a couple of hours. And as for beds…"

"I know, I know. I'm sorry I went on," Clare said, then gripped Jan's arm more tightly. "Do you see who I see?"

A red-haired girl was talking to a tired-looking doctor. She was gesticulating anxiously.

"Jessica Griffiths," Jan said. "But she doesn't look like there's anything wrong with her."

The doctor was following Jessica out of the hospital.

"Go after her," Clare said. "I'll wait here."

Jan hurried out. The doctor was leaning into a taxi. Jessica was talking to him.

"I'm telling you, his leg's broken! I dialled 999, but they couldn't say how long an ambulance would be, so I phoned for a taxi and the driver helped get him in the car."

"All right," the doctor said. "We'll get him a wheelchair in a moment. But first, Mr … Roberts, why don't you tell me where it hurts."

"I'll tell him where it's going to hurt," Jan interrupted. "You're under arrest, both of you: escaping and aiding and abetting an escape."

The taxi driver looked mortified. "I didn't know—"

Jessica Griffiths seized the moment to run off into the dark hospital grounds. Jan let her go. She was small fry. Griffiths was the one they wanted.

"Don't worry," she told the taxi driver. "You're not in trouble. Help me get this prisoner into the squad car, would you? It doesn't look like he'll be running anywhere else in a hurry."

"This man may have a broken leg," the doctor said. "I advise—"

"You can come with us if you want," Jan said, as

the three of them moved Griffiths into the back seat of her panda, "look after him on the way. Otherwise, the prison doctor will assess what to do with him when we get him back there."

"I have fifteen more patients waiting."

"Well, then," Jan said, as Clare hobbled into view. "Off you go."

She pointed out the depressed, uncomfortable-looking Griffiths to Clare. "Look who I've got in the back seat. Think we need to cuff him?"

Julie's front door took a long time to open. Ben thought he heard moving about inside. Why would anyone be up at this time of night? Then, as the door opened, he heard Tammy crying. That explained it.

"Oh," Julie said. "It's you. What are you doing here?"

"I was passing," Ben said, confused. It seemed that she was expecting someone, but not him. "I saw your light on, guessed you were up. Any chance of a cup of tea?"

"Of course," she said, kissing him on the cheek when the door was fully closed. "I'm sorry, you gave me a scare, calling in the middle of the night."

"You said I could call any time."

"Of course. But I thought you were coming after you shift … did you try to phone?" There was something odd about her tone, Ben thought. He had been working up to mentioning the phone, but she'd pre-empted him.

"I did," he said. "It was engaged." Upstairs, the baby still cried.

"Aren't you going to go to her?" he asked.

"After I've put the kettle on."

That wasn't like Julie either. Tammy always came first. Ben thought he heard someone moving around upstairs. While Julie was in the kitchen, Ben went up, remembering the first time he had come to this house, a few short weeks ago. Julie was with another man then, a lad, really. If anyone had told Ben then that ... the person moving about was in Shirley's bedroom. How come?

Ben went into Julie's bedroom and picked up Tammy, but she didn't stop crying. He took her down. Nervously Julie took the baby from him. He made the tea.

"I guess she wants feeding," Julie said.

"Early, isn't it?" Ben asked, as Julie gave Tammy a bottle. He knew Tammy's feeding routine pretty well by now.

"Yes, but it's been noisy – a lot of police sirens. They woke me up."

"The prison break. Three men got out. We haven't caught any of them yet."

"They're not going to be round here, are they?"

Ben decided not to tell her about the car that Gary was guarding.

"There was someone in your mum's room when

I went upstairs. She hasn't come back, has she?"

"No," Julie said, "she's not. Curt must be sleeping in there. He does, sometimes. The bed's better than his. I'd've moved in there myself, only Tammy…"

"I know," Ben told her. "You told me before. Are you all right? You seem…" He was interrupted by a message on his radio.

"*A motel manager in Leicesterhire reports that two men booked in just before midnight, but three men were seen leaving just before two, driving a dark-coloured Peugeot 405, heading towards Nottingham.*"

Why would the escapers come back to Nottingham? Ben wondered. Julie sipped her tea. She hadn't answered his question, Ben realized. Despite – or perhaps because of – the baby in her arms, she looked desperately young.

"What's wrong?" he said.

Julie burst into tears. He held her, the two of them cradling Tammy as she fed.

"I can't tell you," Julie replied. "I want to, but I can't."

"Is it…?"

"Don't start guessing," she said. "You'd only make things worse. It's nothing to do with you and me. Now I think you'd better leave."

"No," Ben said. "Not when…"

Julie pulled away from him.

"I'm asking you to leave," she said. "Don't make me tell you."

She'd gone cold on him. It was less than five hours since they'd come close to making love. Confused and upset, Ben got up.

"When can I see you again?" he asked.

"Leave it until the weekend," she said. It was only Wednesday.

"No," she corrected herself. "Call me after you get up tomorrow. I mean, today. I'll explain if I can. Don't be upset."

"I'm not upset," Ben said. "I'm…" But he saw the pathetic look on her face and thought better of explaining himself further. "Call me if you need to," he added. "Any time."

There was danger, Ben was sure of it. He crossed the street and looked up at the front bedroom window before going back to the car. No movement. Who was in there? What if they were all hiding in Julie's house? It didn't bear thinking about.

"All right," Curt said. "He's gone." Joe breathed a sigh of relief. Julie came into the room.

"That was terrible," she said. "You made me lie to my boyfriend. You've got to leave, now."

"I can't!" Joe protested. "They're outside, in the street. They have to be, otherwise how come they saw that policeman?"

His mobile began to ring again. Julie swore.

"I want you out! This isn't my problem."

"So go to bed!" Curt said. "Leave us to sort this out."

"Even if you get us all killed?" Julie protested.

The phone still rang. Julie held out her hand. "Give it to me!"

She answered the phone. Joe could only hear her side of the conversation.

"Thank you for the warning," she said. "What did he want? A bit of the other, if you must know. He's my boyfriend… Yeah, well, if you'd got through to Eddie, you'd have known… All right. Don't believe me. It's no skin off my nose… Shouldn't you be getting out of here? The place is crawling with police. They've got a description of your car. I don't want you arrested outside my house. It'd be bad for me and bad for my boyfriend, understand?"

It was quite a performance that Curt's sister was putting on, like she was used to dealing with guys like this. But Joe only half listened to her, for Curt was gesturing to him.

"Give me the coat!" he whispered. "Eddie's coat. Come on."

Curt put the coat on.

"Where's the car?"

Joe told him.

"Give me the keys."

"They're in the Mondeo," Joe told him, "but the police are bound to be watching it."

"Doesn't matter," Curt told him. "I'll be the decoy. As soon as they follow me out, you get going. Here, this is all the money I've got."

Joe didn't know how to thank him. "But … you might get hurt."

Curt laughed. On the phone, Julie was saying "Look, why don't you forget Joe? He's not going to testify against you, and he doesn't trust you enough to take your money. So let him get lost. Go and join Eddie. Why should he be the only one who gets a place in the sun?"

She covered the mouthpiece and spoke to Curt. "Where the hell do you think you're going?"

He put a finger to his lips. "Back soon. Keep talking."

"You don't mess with these guys," she said, uncovering the mouthpiece. 'I've got to go," she said. "I'm sorry. I tried. Just do me a favour. Leave me and my brother alone. We never wanted anything to do with this."

She handed the phone over to Joe. On the other end of the line, Chris was still talking.

"He's in your house, sweetheart. Now I'm going to give you a minute, then we're coming in. Understand?"

Joe switched the phone off and put it in his pocket. Curt handed him a torn old leather jacket: not too warm, but black as the night and better than nothing.

"Good luck!" he said, and ran downstairs.

"Curt!" Julie called after him. "You can't. It's too dangerous."

The two of them looked out of the window as Curt, with the hood up, ran out into the street, turned right and picked up pace. Further down the street, a dark-coloured car started its engine and headed after him, with its lights off. Julie turned to Joe.

"Get out!" she said. "Get out and don't come back."

"I'm going, I promise."

Joe hurried downstairs, opened the front door and ran for his life.

16

"Everything all right?" Gary asked, as Ben returned to the car at a quarter to four.

"I'm not sure," Ben said. As he was getting back into the patrol car, a hooded figure came running around the corner.

"He matches the description from earlier," Gary said. "The cheek of him! He's getting into the—"

"Are the keys still in there?" Ben asked.

"Course they are." Gary started the panda's engine, silently cursing Ben for arriving at exactly the wrong moment. The lad was starting the car. Instead of running over, catching him, they would have to block the road and risk damaging the patrol car.

But the lad in the Mondeo was too quick for

them. Before Gary was in gear, he'd started the car and set off down the road, whizzing towards the embankment. Ben radioed it in.

"We're in pursuit of a brown Mondeo, driven by a person in a dark parka coat, matching the description of one who attacked PC Coppola earlier tonight. Heading…

"Hey!" he said to Gary. "What's that?"

They'd reached the end of the road and another car was coming towards them, a dark-coloured Peugeot which matched the description on the radio. A glance in the mirror told Ben who was inside it: the motorway team – or – at least two of them; the third was probably in the rear. Ben called for back-up as the brown Mondeo skidded on to some grass, did a hundred-and-eighty-degree turn on the handbrake, then shot back between the two cars.

"Neat driving!" Gary said. "I didn't know Joe Hatton was in the joy-riding scene."

"He isn't," Ben said, as Gary turned the car round. "But I know a boy who is."

Brett Griffiths was returned to the prison at ten to four in the morning. Neil, along with DCI Charlton and DC Church, was waiting to interview him. Neil met the car at the gate.

"He's asking for a doctor," Clare said. "Suspected broken leg."

"He can see the prison doctor when we've finished questioning him," Neil said. "Are you all right? You look like you're in pain."

Clare gave him one of her brave smiles. "Just an ankle injury. But I might be off work for a while. I've got to go home now. Put it on ice. Good luck with the interview."

With Jan's help, Neil hauled Brett Griffiths out of the car and on to a stretcher. Then they took him to an interview room in the main wing of the prison.

"I'm not saying anything until I see a doctor," Griff told them. He was twenty-two, but looked older. He had the gauntness which Neil associated with hard drugs users, or maybe he just looked that way because it was four in the morning.

"You're wasting your time," he added. "I've nothing to say."

"Why don't you let us be the judge of that?" Phil Church said.

Neil started the questioning. "You've been Joe Hatton's cell-mate for the last couple of weeks, haven't you?"

"So?"

"So whose idea was it to escape, yours or his?"

"No comment."

"I'm sure not much passes you by, Griff."

"Brett," he spat at Neil. "It's only 'Griff' to my friends."

"And Joe was one of them, wasn't he?"

"You've got to be friends when you share a cell, haven't you?"

"Then why did you drop him in it, Griff? Because that's what happened – the motorway team were behind the escape, weren't they? And they wanted Joe dead. We've been talking to other people in your block, Griff. They say you were always spinning Joe silly yarns about your life outside, how you were going to go to London, be a big dealer. Is that what you told him, Griff? Escape with me and I'll show you a good time outside?"

Griff looked a little rattled, but only a little. "Look," he said. "I don't know anything. Me going was an accident. The guard was only meant to take Joe and Gordon but I was with Joe when he came for him, so I went as well. If I'd planned to escape I'd have had money, somewhere to go. I wouldn't have been wandering round Radford in the middle of the night. Now, please can I see a doctor? My leg's giving me agony."

Phil Church shook his head. "I'll tell you what, though. Start telling the truth and we'll let you have some painkillers."

Neil went on. "Joe wouldn't have escaped unless you were going with him. But you were always going to betray him, weren't you? It was a set-up, and when Joe's body is found, it won't just be your remission you lose, not just a couple of years added to your sentence for escaping, oh no. You'll be an accessory to murder. Is that what you want?"

Griffiths' face showed traces of anxiety now. "I've got nothing to do with murder," he said.

"Then you'd better start talking," Neil told him. "I'll give you five minutes to think about it."

Church and Neil went outside, where they joined the two inspectors. "You took a few wild guesses there," Greasby told Neil.

"I wouldn't say *wild*," Neil defended himself. "That's why the boys from Birmingham are here, after all – the motorway team have to be the ones who helped Joe get out. The escape was too well organized to be amateur."

"Your lad's right," Charlton said. "What we need to know is, who was their contact with outside?"

"If Joe Hatton's already dead," Church commented, "I don't see how knowing that makes any difference to anything."

"Maybe not," Charlton said. "But take my word for it, this Griffiths knows something. We've got to make it clear to him that – whatever information he has – the sell-by date's tonight. Agreed?"

"Agreed," DI Greasby said. "Time for you and me to take over the questioning." Disappointed, Neil remained outside to watch.

"We've got to get away from here," Tim told Chris and Kev, who were in the front seat.

"And leave him to the police?" Chris said. "No way. We might as well give ourselves up now, sign a confession. Where do you think he's heading, Kev? Along the river?"

"He's not got much choice, has he?"

"Let me out, then," Tim told the others. "I've had enough."

"Can't stop now," Chris told him, as the boy ahead did an unexpected turn, forcing Kev to brake sharply. "We'd lose him. Anyway, this is your car, isn't it?"

Through the screech of brakes, Chris began to shout at Tim. "All we're doing is protecting our assets. The kid's stolen the car with the mobile phone in it. We came here to try and get it back. He started playing silly beggars. That's our story. It'll stand up in court. Not that it'll ever get there."

Chris had gone mad, Tim decided. The police would find something to do them for. Dangerous driving, for a start.

"What about the gun?" he asked, as Kev skidded round another corner. "How're you going to explain that? How're you going to explain shooting him?"

"We might not need to shoot him," Chris said.

The road ahead, by the Trent Bridge Inn, was blocked by two police cars, blue lights flashing. The Mondeo did another rapid turn.

"Get him in the river!" Chris ordered Kev.

"Easier said than done," Kev commented, but he

reversed, blocking the Mondeo's chance of turning left, back into the Meadows. A police car was coming towards it. Rather than go into the patrol car, or into Kev's car, the Mondeo swerved to the left, mounting the grass embankment.

"Now!" Chris ordered. "Come on!"

Kev skidded across the road, nearly hitting the Mondeo as it tried to remount the road. Then he braked, bringing the car to a stop just where the grass became narrow. Tim yelled. The Mondeo was going to hit the back of him. He didn't have his seat belt on. He would be…

"Yes!" Chris said.

Instead of hitting their car, the Mondeo tried to keep going, along where the strip of grass was at its thinnest. The car shook as it brushed them. For a moment, Tim thought that the lad, balancing on his right-hand wheels, was going to make it back on to the road. Then gravity did its work and the car toppled over.

"Has it gone in the river?" Kev asked.

"Can't tell," Chris said. "Want to make sure?"

Tim didn't wait for the decision. He got out of the car and watched as the Mondeo crashed on to the steep steps between the grass and the river. It teetered for a moment or two, then fell, upside down, into the cold water. The sound of sirens filled the air. Tim heard Kev saying to Chris, "Toss the gun in the water!" followed by a soft *plop*. Then

Tim could bear it no more and ran down to the Mondeo which, any moment, would sink into the Trent, making it much harder to get the driver out.

Half of the car was still out of the water. Tim could see the edge of the driver's door, but not inside it. Water was flooding in. The door hadn't even been properly closed. Any second now, the weight of the water would drag the car into the deep, dark Trent. Tim pulled the door open and reached for the youth inside. He must be mad. This boy could testify against him. But he didn't want another death on his conscience.

The youth wasn't wearing a seat belt. Tim tugged at him the best he could, but it was an awkward angle, and he had difficulty getting the body out. Suddenly, a searchlight came on, nearly blinding him. A black policeman was at his side.

"Trying to finish the job off, are you?" the guy said.

Tim shook his head. "He's stuck. If you could grab his shoulders, I'll try to yank his feet loose."

Somehow, between them, they did it. As the boy's limp body came out, the car lurched backwards. Another officer wrested the boy from him, as though Tim was still a threat. Tim watched the car's slow descent into the dark waters. When a few bubbles were all that remained, someone turned the searchlight off. Tim looked round. The policeman who had helped him was giving the youth the kiss of life. Only when his white partner took over did Tim see the face hidden beneath the hood.

It wasn't Joe Hatton. It was someone else.

"What did you do that for?" the black officer asked him. "You did your level best to get him into the river."

"Not me," Tim told him.

"We watched. You gave him no choice but to crash into you or drive into the river."

"I'm not the one to ask about driving. I was in the back seat, a passenger."

An ambulance was coming, together with more police cars.

"I'm going to take you in," the officer said, then handcuffed Tim and put him in the back of a car.

"What's the charge?"

"Search me! Reckless endangerment will do for a start."

He was about to go. "Hold on!" Tim said. "Will the boy live?"

"The boy's name is Curt. And your guess is as good as mine. Now, you'll have to wait there. I need to find a senior officer."

Tim watched as the police took in Chris and Kev, both protesting that they just happened to be passing. Everything had gone pear-shaped. Tim should never have come along. The others hadn't really needed him, after all. He could have gone off earlier, like Eddie. Kev was there to do the driving. Chris was meant to be doing the persuading. But Chris had lied to Tim. He'd said that they'd get the kid out before the police convinced him to testify. They'd pay him off, then persuade him to disappear. Tim had been naïve. It was only when they got the boy into the garage that he realized what kind of persuasion Chris really had in mind.

Would Tim have let Chris kill the kid if Joe Hatton hadn't done a runner? He didn't know. Chris had worked himself into such a state, he might have killed Tim as well. And if he hadn't done it then, he'd certainly want to do it now, after Tim jumped out of that car. The black policeman was coming back. Tim had to think hard. How much was he going to tell them?

Despite the presence of two inspectors, Griff was still giving nothing away. Neil interrupted the interview to tell his superiors the news.

"They're bringing in the motorway team," he said, when Greasby was outside. "All three of them tried to run Curt Wilder into the river, but one of them turned hero and saved his life. We might be able to drive a wedge between them."

"Why Curt Wilder?" DCI Charlton asked, as they made the short drive back to Oxclose Lane Police Station. "Where's Joe Hatton?"

"Evidently they thought it was Hatton in the car. We don't know where Joe is yet."

"At least we're the only ones looking," Phil Church said.

"Not necessarily," Neil commented, "not if the motorway team have a corrupt officer in their pocket."

"True," Greasby said. "Maybe we should talk to Griffiths again before we interrogate Jennings, Stevens and Hunter."

As he spoke, two cars arrived. The three men were brought in. They were smartly dressed. Only one of them looked dishevelled: he must be Jennings, the one who'd gone in the river. The other two, older men looked defiant.

"Keep them apart at all times," Greasby ordered.

He and Charlton saw that this was done.

"You coming back to the prison?" Neil asked Phil.

"Not me. I want to sit in on the motorway team interviews."

"Me too," Neil agreed, enthusiastically, "when I get back."

"That Tim Jennings looks like he might be about to break. I want to be there when it happens."

"You mean *if*," Neil corrected him, optimistically. "Do you really think he'll…?"

"I expect it depends on what kind of deal the Chief Inspector can offer him."

Neil thought about Phil's words as he drove back to

the prison with Greasby. What kind of deal could the police offer Griffiths, or Tim Jennings? Their hands were tied much more thoroughly than in the old days. You couldn't drop charges, only make requests for a lenient sentence, which, normally, the judge would go along with. But, for that to happen, the evidence they got from either man would have to be cast iron, because the motorway team were bound to have the best lawyers money could buy. Estimates of their takings over the last two years topped ten million.

Griff had his leg strapped up.

"He ought to be in the hospital wing," the prison doctor told Greasby. "It's broken in two places."

"Tough," Greasby said. He and Neil had a brief discussion about their questioning tactics, then walked back into the interview room. Griff began to whinge about the pain.

"We've captured the motorway team," Greasby informed him, interrupting the moans. "There are new charges against them which will ensure that each one of them is put away for a long time."

Neil wasn't sure how true this was, but the Inspector knew what he was doing.

"Therefore," he said, "you have nothing to fear from those men, only from the police officer who we know is working with them. We need your help. We need you to tell us who this corrupt officer is."

Griff shook his head. "I don't know what you're talking about," he said.

Neil and Greasby looked at each other. Did the corrupt officer exist, or was he just a figment of Neil's imagination? Greasby looked at his watch before speaking again.

"We're going back to interview the team in five minutes," he said. "Either you tell us what we want to know now and we drop all extra charges against you, or I'll make sure your sentence is doubled. That's the choice. What's the answer?"

Griff stared at them both for a moment, trying to see if they were bluffing. Finally, his face fell into a resigned expression.

"All right," he said. "Get me a solicitor to OK the deal and I'll tell you what you want to know."

Julie couldn't sleep until Curt got home. She heard noises: screeches, sirens, stuff that went bump in the night. If she'd had a choice, she wouldn't have let Curt go. It was too dangerous, pretending to be Joe. Tammy apart, Curt was all the family she had left. It looked like her daughter was going to be permanently deprived of a grandmother. She couldn't do without an uncle as well.

Finally, it came, as she'd known it would: not Curt, but the knock on the door. It wasn't Ben's knock, but her boyfriend was there, standing next to Gary, the sandy-haired officer who he usually patrolled with.

"Can we come in?" her boyfriend's partner asked.

"Is it Curt? What's happened to him?"

Ben sat her down while Gary put the kettle on.

"Why didn't you tell me what was going on?" he asked.

"I couldn't. I just couldn't."

"Why not?"

Julie took a deep breath. There were so many explanations. All she wanted was to know what had happened to Curt. It was cruel of him not to tell her.

"They were outside," she told Ben. "All right? They had a gun, Joe said. They might have hurt you, and me, and Joe, and Curt. What's happened to Curt?"

"He'll live," Ben said. "They've taken him to the hospital."

"Did they shoot him?"

"No."

As Gary brought the tea out, Ben explained how Curt had ended up in the river. He had broken ribs and probably a fractured skull: the result of not wearing a seat belt. But he was going to survive.

"Do you know where Joe is?" Ben asked.

"No. He left as soon as Curt was gone, in the opposite direction."

"What was he wearing?"

Julie couldn't lie to Ben. She told him.

"Did he have any money?"

"Not much. Curt gave him what he had. It can't have been more than a fiver. And he had a mobile phone. Actually, that belonged to one of the motorway team, the driver."

"Do you know the number?" Gary.

"Sorry."

"Do you know where he was going?" Ben again.

"He didn't know where he was going himself. He didn't have anywhere to go."

They'd both run out of questions, but looked at each other to confirm that there was nothing left to say.

"Which hospital have they taken Curt to?" Julie asked, though she knew that she wouldn't be able to visit him, because there was no one to look after Tammy.

"Queen's. It's probably too soon for them to be able to tell you anything. The doctor said that you can call after six."

"Thanks for finding out for me."

Gary stood up. "We'd better be going," he said. "Join the hunt for Joe Hatton. He can't be that far away."

Julie looked at Ben. "Could you give us a minute?" he asked his partner.

"I need the loo anyway." He looked at Julie.

"Upstairs, on the left."

When Gary was gone she turned to Ben. He didn't hold her, or stroke her, or do any of the things that she wanted him to do. He had a face on him like thunder. She'd never seen him that way before.

"Am I in trouble?" she asked.

"He's an escaped prisoner," Ben said.

"I didn't know he was here until just before you came," she said, which was nearly true. She didn't want to tell a lie to Ben. "And those men were outside."

"I'll write it up," Ben said. "I doubt we'll charge you. But I'm not so sure about Curt."

"He was trying to save Joe's life. He had nothing to do with him escaping."

"I believe you, but he stole a car."

"It belonged to one of the motorway team."

"Makes no odds. He's only fifteen. He's got no licence, or insurance, and lots of previous for the same offence. What if he'd killed someone?"

"The only person he's ever hurt is himself."

Ben shrugged both shoulders. Julie could hear Gary coming back downstairs.

"What about us?" she asked. "Are we over?"

Ben stared at her. There was fear in his eyes. He was trying to be hard, she could tell, but failing. "I don't know," he said. "I don't know whether I'll be in trouble for keeping quiet about my relationship with you."

"Will you come by later, when the shift's over?" Julie begged.

"I'll come if I can," Ben said. "But be patient.

They might make us do overtime."

Gary walked back into the room and Ben stood up. He left without kissing her, without even saying "goodbye".

Julie felt ashamed, because she was more worried about losing Ben than she was about the state of her brother. She wished that she had her mum to talk to. But Mum was out of reach. She went back up to bed. *I will not cry*, she ordered herself. *I'll be strong. I'll go to sleep.* But she could not sleep, only count the minutes until she was allowed to ring up about Curt, until Ben's shift ended.

17

Joe sat by the canal, listening to the night traffic go by. He'd come this way, back into the city, because he was sure that the police would pursue him along the banks of the Trent. It stood to reason. You could get out of the city that way. But it was easier to get lost in the city than it was outside it. He'd only been caught before because he took a bus to the countryside, hid in a hut and made himself a sitting duck.

He should be dead by now. Joe didn't know what he'd done to deserve a friend like Curt. He'd betrayed his best friend, Dean Sutherland, and had no idea where the footballer was living at the moment. But Dean would never have risked his life for Joe, the way Curt had.

Sirens sounded, all of them distant. A while back, there'd been an ambulance. He got out the mobile phone and switched it on. A green light flashed slowly, indicating that the battery level was low. Joe thought about calling the motorway team. But what was the point? No matter what they offered, he could never trust them. He thought about calling Julie Wilder. But she had no reason to talk to him. He thought about calling his mum. She would be asleep, and would probably swear at him if he woke her up, even if it was only to say goodbye.

An animal was padding by. The moon appeared between the clouds and Joe saw not one, but two, three, four – a whole family of foxes crossing the path into the bushes. For some reason, they made him feel happy. If they could survive in the rough, near a city, so could he. But Joe didn't have to live in the wild. He stood up and began to walk, having realized, finally, what he had to do.

Neil wasn't allowed to join the Brett Griffiths interview when it resumed.

"Sorry, Neil," DI Greasby told him. "Too many cooks and all that…"

Neil had been about to go back into the interview room when Phil Church appeared. "My boss insists on someone from the task force being in on the interview," he said, then added, for Neil's benefit, "I'd rather be interviewing Chris Stevens."

"You did a really good job earlier," Greasby told Neil. "It won't be forgotten." Neil wished that he believed this.

"You can watch, or get back over to Oxclose Lane," Greasby told him. "It's up to you."

"I'll stick around for a few more minutes, then get over there," Neil said. He wanted to see the beginning of this interview, to find out whether Griffiths would finally give up what he knew.

But the beginning was disappointing. When Church and Greasby sat down, Griffiths shuffled in his chair, whispered to his solicitor, and then closed his eyes.

"My client has nothing to add to his previous statement," the solicitor said. "So, if there are no further questions, I suggest you provide him with medical attention immediately."

Angrily, Greasby began to grill Griffiths again. Outside the room, Neil listened for a minute, then asked to speak to the governor. When he got hold of her, he requested some information.

"I'll need to check that," she said. "It'll take a while. Do you want to wait?"

"No," Neil said. "Call me, please. I'll be at Oxclose Lane."

Before he could leave, Phil Church and DI Greasby came out. The DI looked at Neil and shook his head. "I thought we had him."

"Earlier, he more or less confirmed that one of

the people in our squad or Brum is a bent copper," Neil said.

"Not that line again," Church complained. "There's no evidence that—"

"Listen," Neil interrupted. "There've been situations in this investigation where a leak's occurred. The most recent was over the surveillance of Eddie Broom's house on Radcliffe Road. Whoever tipped the motorway team off had to be a police officer."

"And whoever shot Paul Grace might have had operational knowledge for that evening," Phil Church commented. "But only *might*. All of our officers have been scrutinized thoroughly. If there is a snitch, he or she's one of yours."

Neil said nothing. He thought that any leak was more likely to be from Birmingham – no Nottingham officer knew everything about the task force's operation. And the mole - if there was one – might even be someone quite senior. The motorway team had enough money to tempt someone of a rank up to and beyond that of DCI Charlton.

Tim Jennings sat in a cell, waiting. He still didn't know what the charges against him, if any, were. The agreement was that, whenever they got arrested, they didn't speak until their solicitor got there. But Tim was at odds with the other members of the team, so their solicitor would no longer be his. On legal matters, Tim wasn't used to thinking for himself. He didn't know how to play this one at all.

The custody sergeant came and unlocked him. "A detective's ready to see you now."

Just a detective. Not the Chief Inspector. Not even a sergeant. Tim wondered what their game was.

DC Foster was a young man, too: slightly built, for a copper, with fairish hair and a Nottingham accent. He had a shifty look, as though he wasn't really supposed to be here.

"I've come to talk to you because you pulled that lad out of the car," he told Tim.

"Who was he?" Tim asked, making conversation, trying to suss the detective out.

"Curt Wilder. A mate of Joe Hatton's."

"And is he…?"

"He'll live. Why did you do it? You thought he was Joe, didn't you?"

Tim nodded. No point in denying that.

"For the tape recorder, please."

"Yes," Tim said. "I thought he was Joe Hatton. But I couldn't let him die."

"Even though he was a potential witness against you?"

Tim didn't reply. No point in incriminating himself.

"You see, I'm confused," Neil said. "You saved Curt's life, thinking he was Hatton, yet you had Inspector Grace killed."

"That had nothing to do with me."

"Really? You and your chums were the ones who benefited."

"Even so," Tim told the detective, "I didn't know it was going down, I swear."

"Who did know?" DC Foster snapped back.

Tim didn't answer. "I think I need to speak to a lawyer," he said, eventually. "Consider my options very carefully."

"You want the same solicitor your friends are waiting for?" Foster asked.

"I guess…"

"Because the way it looks to me is that they're going to blame everything on you. You're the back seat driver, the guy controlling the whole gang. You're—"

"It's not true!" Tim protested. "I'm the youngest. I do what I'm told. I never wanted anyone killed. It was part of the original deal. No one gets badly hurt."

He stopped speaking. The detective was winding him up. Nobody would really suggest that Tim was the leader of the team. When you got right down to it, he was the dogsbody, the dispensable one … but could he prove it? Maybe the DC was right. The others would try to blame everything on him.

"Do you want to make a deal with us?" the detective asked.

Tim hesitated. "Maybe. I'm gonna have to think about it, get some advice."

The detective stood up. "I need one thing from you, a gesture of good faith, if you like."

"What?"

DC Foster leant forward, so that he was almost breathing on Tim. "We know that you have a mole in the police force. That's how you avoided being raided in West Bridgford. That's how you knew when Inspector Grace would be coming home."

Tim nodded. There was no point denying it. The detective seemed to suppress a smile, then gave him a hard look.

"Who is it?"

Tim shook his head. "I don't know. I've never known."

If Tim *had* known the name, he wouldn't have told the detective. He needed some information to cut a deal with. But this was one piece he didn't have.

"I'm telling the truth," he protested. "It was part of the contract we had with the policeman – for security, that's what Eddie said. When Eddie went abroad, he told Chris. Kev and I had no idea who he was. Not the rank, nothing."

"*He?*"

"Yes. It's a bloke."

The detective clenched his hand on the table. "You must know this, then. Where's the bloke from? Nottingham or Birmingham?"

For a moment, Tim considered holding on to the

information. It was too valuable to give away just like that. But the detective was in his face, and Tim had said too much already.

"It's obvious, innit?" Tim said. "If he was from Nottingham, I wouldn't be talking to you now. The guy's a Brummie."

Tim felt the detective's sigh of relief blow against his face. Then the interview room door opened abruptly. "DC Foster, I want to speak to you immediately!" said a man with a loud, bossy Birmingham accent.

"What the hell do you think you're playing at?" DCI Charlton asked Neil. "This is the apex of a major investigation. You charge in and start questioning a key witness without a by-your-leave..."

Neil kept his cool. "How much did you hear?" he asked.

"I didn't hear anything. When I finished trying to get the others to talk I came out to find that you were in with Jennings, supposedly with my permission."

"I had to say that," Neil said.

"I'll have your job," the DCI threatened. "But first I want to hear your explanation."

"I've got an explanation," Neil said. "But I can't tell it to you yet."

He picked up the phone and dialled the switchboard. There hadn't been any calls for him. Neil was in a dilemma. Should he wait for the prison governor to confirm what he already suspected, or should he tell DCI Charlton now? There was a chance that the DCI himself was the mole. In which case, Neil didn't know what to do. Go through Greasby, who was Charlton's inferior? Get the superintendent or the Chief Constable out of his bed? Find Charlton's superior officer in Birmingham?

The phone rang, saving him the decision. The prison governor told him what he had expected to hear. "Thanks," Neil said when she'd finished, "and would you mind finding DI Greasby and getting him to call me straightaway?"

"What the hell is going on?" Charlton asked, as Neil put the phone down.

"Griffiths was about to tell us who the police mole was," Neil informed him. "But then Phil Church replaced me on the interview, at your request."

"That's right."

"Was it his suggestion?"

"It was, as a matter of fact, but I don't…" A cloud crossed the Chief Inspector's face. He was beginning to see. Neil continued.

"I came over here and questioned Timothy Jennings. I couldn't seek your authorization because it was possible that you were in the pay of the motorway team. Jennings didn't know who the mole was, but he did know that the mole was a Brummie."

Charlton said nothing. Neil went on. "Before I

returned to Oxclose Lane, I asked the prison governor to check the visiting records of Joe Hatton and Brett Griffiths. As I expected, both of you had interviewed Joe, alone and together, several times, and the two of you had interviewed Griffiths, but only once."

"That's right. When he started sharing a cell with Hatton we wanted him to give us information about the boy's movements, but he wouldn't cooperate."

"I think he cooperated in the end," Neil said. "You see, Phil Church went to see Brett Griffiths twice more, the week before the escape."

"But he was meant to be..."

"Visiting Hatton. I think it was Church who acted as go-between for the motorway team. I reckon Griffiths coordinated the escape from inside the prison, telling Loscoe and Hatton what was going on, tempting Joe to join them. But Church is our mole."

Charlton looked flustered, angry. "Do you have any *proof*?" he asked.

"We could get some," Neil said. "Church was keen to be on the interviews with both Stevens and Jennings. We could try and arrange for him and Stevens to be alone in a room together, bug him. Aside from that, there's Stevens' mobile phone records, and there's Griffiths. If we interview Griff without Church present, he might give him up."

"And he might not," Charlton said. "I'm finding

this very hard to believe. Phil's one of our best officers. He just passed his sergeant's exams."

"If I'm right," Neil said, "he's also responsible for Paul Grace's death."

The phone rang. It was DI Greasby. Neil handed it over to Charlton.

"Don't let that solicitor go," the Chief Inspector told the Inspector. "We need to interview Griffiths one more time. But you needn't inform Phil Church. Tell Phil he's wanted back at the station, to help interview Christopher Stevens. Oh, and I'm returning Neil Foster to you. He'll fill you in on what's going on."

He put the phone down and looked at Neil. "I hope to God you're wrong," he said.

18

The phone rang just after five. Julie was awake, watching shadows on the wall. She expected it to be Ben. Or maybe she hoped it was. She dreaded the call being from the hospital, telling her that Curt's condition was more serious than they'd first thought – not just a fracture, but brain damage, maybe. She picked up the receiver with trepidation.

"Julie? It's Joe. Listen, I haven't got long. The batteries on this phone are about to run out. Did Curt get back OK?"

Julie almost laughed. "He's in hospital with two broken ribs and a fractured skull. The police and the motorway team between them managed to run him into the river. It's a miracle he survived."

A silence at the other end. Then, "I'm really,

really sorry."

"What did you ever do for him?" Julie asked. "What did you do to make Curt think you were worth dying for?"

"Nothing," Joe said, "but I'll make it up to you one day, I promise."

"You can make it up by staying out of our lives," Julie told him.

"Listen, Julie, you're great. I've always thought you were great."

"I don't want to hear this," Julie said.

"I just wanted to tell you…"

The line began to crackle and splutter. He must be under a bridge or something, Julie thought. Then it went dead. Batteries, she remembered, and put the phone down. What had he wanted to tell her? She didn't care. There was nothing that she wanted to hear, nothing at all, expect for the sound of Ben's voice, telling her that it was still all right: they were meant to be together.

She lay in her cold bed, watching the walls, and waited.

"For the last time, my client has nothing—"

"He was on the verge of telling us something earlier," Neil interrupted, "before DC Church came along. Church made two visits to you in the last fortnight, Griff, didn't he? Why?"

The prisoner gave a cocky smile. "He wanted me

to find out what Joe was gonna do about the motor-way team. I wouldn't tell him."

Neil shook his head. "Let me refresh your memory. In the first interview there was a chief inspector present. He wanted you to tell him what Joe was saying when he was in his cell. But the other two meetings were about something else altogether."

Griffiths said nothing. Neil went on.

"Come on, Griff, we've already worked it out. The guy we're talking about is going to go down. He's being set up as we speak. In half an hour's time, we won't need you. We'll have him incrimi-nating himself on tape. Give him up now and we'll drop the new charges. It's the best deal you'll ever get."

Griffiths was still silent. DI Greasby spoke. "The motorway team are inside. They're not going any-where. You've nothing to worry about from them."

The prisoner looked at his solicitor as if to see whether he should trust them. The solicitor nodded.

"All right," Griffiths said. "It was Church. He told me what the score was – how it was meant to look like the big deal was getting Loscoe out, but really it was a front. They needed to get Joe. I sounded Joe out, but he wasn't interested in doing a runner. That made Church more anxious. He thought that Joe might be about to talk. He suggested we fixed it so that it looked like an accident, but Joe had to come along."

"Who organized the prison guard's wife being threatened?" Neil asked.

"I don't know. But Church told me it was going down, so he was in on it. Look, does he have to know that I've named him? I mean, that guy has some serious contacts."

"Did Phil Church have Paul Grace killed?" Neil asked.

"As if he'd tell me a thing like that."

It was worth a try, Neil thought. The very idea of a police officer having another one killed sickened him. He wondered whether Church had done it himself. Once someone crossed the line, anything was possible. But, no, Neil remembered: Church was in Scotland when it happened.

"Are we done?" the solicitor asked.

Greasby glanced at Neil. "That's all for now," he said. "Thank you for your eventual cooperation."

Neil hurried to the phone to call Charlton.

"Get back over here," the DCI said. "I've told Phil that you and I are going to interview Hunter, while he and DI Greasby will interview Stevens. Phil Church is meant to wait for John Greasby, but, if Griffiths was telling the truth, I don't think he'll be that patient."

The shift was into its last hour. They'd started in darkness and were ending in darkness. This time of year, when you were on nights, it was possible to miss the daylight completely. Gary had never known a night watch go quicker, but he was still beginning to tire. It would be better if he and Ben had some kind of result. True, the motorway team had been taken tonight, but Gary and Ben had nothing to do with them. Also, the team had been arrested before and got away with it. Why should tonight be any different? They'd just dropped DCI Charlton at the prison. He'd been tight-lipped about the prospect of charges.

"Back to the station?" Gary asked Ben.

"I guess," Ben looked over his shoulder and added, "Funny time for a visit."

A *Yellow Cars* taxi was pulling up. A wiry figure in a torn leather jacket was getting out of it.

"That looks like…" Gary began to say.

"Joe Hatton," Ben finished the sentence for him. They pulled up alongside the escaped prisoner.

"Forgot something?" Gary asked.

"Left my brains behind," Hatton told them, ruefully. "I'm giving myself up. And could you get someone from CID over? I want to be a witness against the motorway team."

19

"**B**ig night," Gary said, when they were finally headed back to the station. By now it was ten to six.

"Swing through the Maynard Estate, would you?" Ben said.

Gary was tactfully silent, but only for a while.

"It's official, then?" Gary asked, as they turned into Julie's road. "You're going out with her?"

Ben said nothing.

"Are you going to tell the boss?" Gary asked.

"I haven't really thought it through yet."

"Looks like someone's beaten you to it."

There was already a police car outside Julie's house.

* * *

John and Ruth stood outside the door.

"You do the talking," John said.

"OK. Think I should ring the bell again?"

"No. I can hear footsteps."

The door was answered by a pale teenage girl in a dressing gown. She looked like she'd been crying. As the door opened, her face momentarily brightened. Ruth had heard about Julie Wilder, but never seen her in the flesh. She'd been expecting her to be slovenly and a bit cheap but there was something vulnerable and almost beautiful about this girl. She seemed sorry to see them.

"Is Ben Shipman not with you?" Julie asked. Odd question.

"No. We're here about your brother, Curt. Is his mother here?"

"No," Julie said. "She's on holiday. How long are they going to keep Curt?"

"At least a week, I believe. Do you have a number where we can contact Curt's mother?"

"No, I don't," Julie said. "Is Curt going to be charged with anything?"

"That's not our decision," Ruth said. "Can you tell us when your mother will be coming home?"

"No," Julie said, looking over Ruth's shoulder. "Oh, thank God you're here!" Ruth turned to see Ben Shipman walking in through the open door. Julie Wilder threw herself around him as though they were lovers who'd been parted for years. Ruth couldn't believe what she was seeing. John put a hand under her elbow, guiding her out.

"Time we were going back to the station." He closed the Wilders' front door behind them.

"There's one young man who keeps his brain in his genitals," John commented. "He's asking for trouble, that Ben Shipman is."

Ruth said nothing, but strode ahead of him, brushing back tears with her hand.

After Griff had told his story, the three CID officers returned to Oxclose Lane. The DCI went to have a word with Phil Church, then returned.

"I've put him in the interview room with Stevens," Charlton told Neil and John Greasby. "He hasn't switched on the tape recorder yet. I told him you were on your way down, so if he's going to make a move, it has to be quick."

"Where's the microphone?" DI Greasby asked.

The interview room was so bare that it was hard to conceal anything.

"It's hidden in the tape machine," Greasby said. "Best place to hide a microphone is where people expect to find one."

They went and watched from outside the room. Church was standing up, walking round the room. It didn't look like he and Stevens were talking, but, without the tape recorder on, the officers couldn't hear what was going on inside.

"Can we hear what the bug's picking up?" Neil asked.

"The equipment's hidden in a store room upstairs."

Neil, Greasby and Charlton crammed into the store room and listened to the conversation as it was taped. Stevens spoke first.

"Is it clean?"

"Far as I can tell."

"How long have we got?"

"Five minutes at most."

"Have they found the kid?" Stevens asked.

"Not yet," Church told him. "But you have to assume that he'll testify when they do."

Stevens swore. "How serious is the other stuff?"

"They might try and make dangerous driving into attempted murder. They won't prove that you organized the escape unless Loscoe testifies against you."

"He should be out of the country by now," Stevens said, then added, "Is Griffiths keeping his trap shut?"

"It was touch and go for a while, but yeah," Church said, his voice wobbling just slightly. "It would have been easier if you'd bunged him a decent wad, like I promised him. Is Tim Jennings solid?"

"You tell me," Stevens replied, in a sneering tone.

"Jennings talked to the DCI earlier, but I don't know what went down. Why did he help to save the boy?"

"Your guess is as good as mine," Stevens said. "I think he's going soft. He went spare when that inspector got done."

There was a pause, during which the three men in the store room waited anxiously to see if Stevens or Church would name the killer.

"We need to be very, very careful," Church said, eventually. "Jennings doesn't know, does he?"

"About you? No. You're in the clear. Any problems, talk to Eddie. He'll see you right. I'll get our brief to sort Tim out."

"You'll do *no comment* interviews all round, yeah?" Church said.

"No."

"What?" Church sounded anxious.

"I'm not saying one word until my brief arrives," Stevens told him. Both men could be heard laughing.

"Have we got enough?" Greasby asked.

"Give it another minute," Charlton told him. "They might still give up the murderer."

"If I give this signal," Church said, "it means that they've picked up Hatton."

"Damn!" Neil said. They should have had somebody watching the room. Now they didn't know what the signal was.

"And how do I know if Tim's given us up?"

"You think that's a serious prospect?" Church asked.

"Depends how bad things look. Tug your other ear, all right?"

Neil, listening, smiled.

"All right," Church said, "I'd better go. Greasby'll arrive any second."

There was a really loud noise, an echoing clank, followed by a small explosion.

"Testing one two three. Testing."

A loud whirr, followed by a resounding click and the same words again, only louder and a repeat of the whirr and the click.

"What are you up to?" Stevens asked.

"It's in case Greasby wants to know what I was doing in here. I've just been making sure that all the equipment's working."

"Nice one," Stevens said.

"Good luck," Phil Church told him.

They heard the door being opened, then locked. "Come on," DI Greasby said.

"It might not hold up in court," Charlton said. "Some of the conversation was ambivalent. There was no mention of money."

"*Talk to Eddie,*" Neil quoted. "*He'll see you right.*"

"We need to take him tonight," Greasby insisted, "before he does any more damage. We'll work out the case against him later."

Phil Church smiled broadly when the three of them marched in to the CID office.

"Oh, there you are, sir," he said to Greasby. "I've got Stevens waiting in an interview room."

"That won't be necessary," DCI Charlton told him.

"Why? Has Kevin Hunter coughed? You weren't in there long."

"I haven't been in yet. Had something to do first."

He held up the tape recorder, rewound it for a few seconds, then let it play. Church's voice came on. "If I give this signal, it means that they've picked up Hatton." Charlton switched it off again.

"How much did they pay you, Phil?"

Church, his chin trembling, was silent. Charlton went on. "You've let me down, Phil. You let everybody down, yourself most of all. You do not have to say anything, but if you do not say now something that is later used in your defence…"

The pupils of Phil Church's eyes darted around, but there was only one door and Neil was blocking it. He'd picked up a pair of handcuffs earlier. Now he got them out.

"Surely not," Church said as Neil stepped forward.

"Put them on," Charlton said. "You're being arrested for conspiracy to murder."

"*Murder?*" Church said, dismissively. "You'll never…"

"Two conspiracies to murder," Charlton interrupted. "We've heard that there was an attempt on Joe Hatton's life earlier tonight. The other one is Inspector Paul Grace."

"I had nothing to do with that!" Church protested. "I was in Glasgow at the time."

"If you didn't do it," Neil said, "then I'll bet you know who did."

Church took a deep breath. "I'm not saying anything else until I see a solicitor."

"Do you have your own, or would you like to share the motorway team's?" Neil enquired, facetiously.

They led him down to the cells.

John Farraday dropped Ruth off just after six. She'd known that tonight was going to be a hard one. Working with Ben was never going to be easy. But having his new relationship thrown in her face like that … and he was going out with a girl six years younger than him, three years younger than Ruth! Julie Wilder might be a tramp, but that didn't make Ruth feel better. She felt worthless – too plain, too small, too sad and stupid to ever get another man. Ben was all she'd ever wanted – a better bloke than she'd ever hoped to win. But at the back of her mind, she'd always known that he would dump her sooner rather than later. And now he had.

Normally, Ruth would have vented all these feelings on Clare, her best friend. But Clare was in a worse position. Somehow, instead of their joint misery bringing them closer together, the two events – Paul's death, Ben's desertion – seemed to cancel each other out. The two friends had hardly talked since Clare came back from the funeral. And now Clare was hurt.

There was no light on in her friend's room. Ruth knocked softly on the door, then opened it. Clare was on the bed in her nightdress, one knee pressed against her chest. Her curtains were open. The only light came from a streetlamp outside, which cast a ghostly hue over the bed. Ruth saw that Clare's left ankle was bandaged and swollen.

"How long have you been home?"

"Hours," Clare said, through clenched teeth. "I didn't want to wake Sam."

"Have they given you pain killers?"

Clare nodded. "And lots of ice. I can't take any more Ibuprofen for another hour."

"Nonsense," Ruth said. "Get some down you. Where are they?"

"Not now." Clare shook her head and began to cry again.

"Talk about it," Ruth said. "Come on, talk to me about it."

She handed Clare some tissues. Clare blew her nose and dried her face. "I've got to tell you," she said. "I've got to tell someone or … or nothing'll ever make any sense again."

"What is it?" Ruth asked.

"You'd split up with Ben and it didn't seem right to say at the time."

"Say it now," Ruth insisted. Telling her about Julie Wilder could wait.

"It was Paul," Clare whispered, as Ruth clenched her hand. "Two days before he died, Paul asked me to marry him. The night he died, I was going to say 'yes'."

She started crying again. "But I never got the chance. I was going to marry him, Ruth, and he never knew. But now I'll never marry anybody. He was the only one for me, and now he's gone."

"Oh, Clare!" Ruth said.

The two women held each other for a long time, until, as dawn began to break, they slept.

The news of Joe Hatton's return and Phil Church's arrest led to a brief bout of jubilation in the CID office. At half six, cold beer was found from somewhere. Neil had some, even though drinking before breakfast made him feel decidedly queasy.

Everything was coming together. Joe's testimony would put extra pressure on Tim Jennings because Joe could identify him as one of the men who burgled Umberto Capricio's house. If CID made a deal with Jennings, the other members of the team were looking at long sentences for multiple burglaries, kidnap, aiding a prisoner to escape and a number of smaller offences. The one thing which they couldn't be charged with was Paul Grace's murder. Phil Church claimed to know nothing about that, and his alibi checked out. He had been getting off a train in Glasgow on the night of Grace's death, looking for Eddie Broom. Other officers had seen him there.

When the rest of the motorway team were convicted, there might be enough evidence to extradite Eddie Broom, or there might not. The chances of finding him were pretty remote anyhow. It didn't matter, Neil thought. Broom was only the reconnaissance man. He didn't take part in any of the burglaries. He could enjoy his retirement with Shirley Wilder.

Paul Grace's killer was almost certainly a professional hitman. Therefore, the police would never catch him, or conclusively prove that the team had employed him. But the judge doing the sentencing would know what they had done. Stevens and Hunter would get maximum sentences on every charge that they were found guilty of. Church, who must have given the motorway team crucial details of Paul Grace's movements, would also go down for a very long stretch.

"Bottoms up!" DCI Charlton said, the first time Neil could recall anyone using that phrase outside a TV set.

"Bottoms up!" the others repeated, and drained their glasses.

Neil wondered how Clare was. He'd heard about her accident and wanted to go to her, but couldn't: because he was busy, because he had a new girl-friend now, and because his presence would be awkward while Clare was in mourning.

"You ought to be celebrating, son," DCI Charlton said, slapping Neil on the back. "Get that down you and have another one. We've had a triumph tonight, a big, bloody triumph."

"He's right," DI Greasby said. "You've done well, Neil."

"Give us a toast," Charlton told him, doling out the last few cans.

Neil hesitated for moment, knowing that the victory – if victory it turned out to be – was far from complete. "Come on," John Greasby said, gently prodding him. Neil's chin wobbled as he held up his glass and spoke in a voice which was much too loud.

"Paul Grace," he said.

"Paul Grace," the others repeated, more quietly, then drank.

EPILOGUE

"You found it all right, then?"

Gordon Loscoe had just got out from the back of the lorry he'd been hiding in since Dover. He laughed. "Where are we exactly?"

"Near the border."

"That's handy. You've done me proud, Eddie."

Eddie put an arm around Gordon's shoulder. "That's what friends are for. Look, I know you could probably do with a shower and everything, after a day on that lorry, but shall we get this business over with first?"

Gordon smiled. "Why not?"

As Eddie drove into Switzerland, he filled Gordon in on what had happened since his escape, thirty-six hours before.

"Chris and Steve are gonna need a good lawyer now," he concluded, "what with Tim turned against them. They're going down for a long time."

"Serves them right," Gordon said, seeming to forget how close Eddie had been to both men. "Stealing's one thing, knocking someone about a bit. But murder … you never went in for that, did you, Eddie?"

"Not me," Eddie said. "I advised them against it. Kept well away from the dirty stuff myself. They'll be drawing their pensions before they get out. No escape from the place they're going to. Still, they'll have a nice big wad waiting in Switzerland to ease their retirement."

"Same as me," Gordon said, as they drove into Geneva.

"You're sure about taking it all out today?"

Gordon beamed. "Absolutely. Maxine must know that the account exists by now. There's a chance that she'll get an injunction, find a way of freezing the money."

"You're positive Interpol won't be waiting for you?"

"Account's in a false name," Gordon assured him. "I'll take my chances."

Eddie waited nervously while Gordon went inside. As far as he knew, there was no warrant out for his own arrest, but if Interpol caught him with Gordon

Loscoe, they would hold him, too. The British police might come up with an excuse to extradite him. If all went well today, Eddie would move on to Spain, then South America. Shirley was anxious to see the world, having lived in a dump for most of her natural. Eddie wanted to show it to her.

Gordon got back into the car, delight etched across his face.

"I got it! Closed the account. It was brilliant. So easy."

He went on like this for some time, describing the life that he was going to have. No gambling or frittering away the money this time. He wanted to go into business with Eddie.

"The car business, like the old days. Only we flog top-notch Rollers and BMWs instead of fiddling the meter on dodgy ex-rentals. What do you say, Eddie?"

"Sounds like a possibility." He turned off into a forest.

"Where are we going?" Gordon asked.

"Little place I want you to see."

They turned up a narrow track and parked in thick woodland. The hole was exactly where Eddie remembered. It hadn't rained since he dug it, so the pit was dry. Not that this would have made much difference. Gordon looked at it.

"Take no chances, eh? Bury your money deep."

"That's right," Eddie said.

"I can't tell you how much I appreciate your help on all this," Gordon said. "I mean, I know we go back a long way, but this goes way beyond any obligation you ought to feel."

"I know," Eddie said, and Gordon caught the strangeness in his tone.

"What is it?" he said.

"You want to know why I helped you? Because of Shirley."

Gordon smiled and began to gush unconvincingly. "Well, Shirley and I go back a long way too. Course we never … you know … you and her are just right for each other. Made to be together."

"You see, your Natalie is going out with Shirley's Curt. And Shirley's sentimental about family."

"Oh." Gordon looked confused. He obviously couldn't care less who Natalie was going out with. "Right."

"And, to be honest, it suited me to get you out. There was someone else I wanted to get over the wall as well."

"The kid," Gordon said. "I wondered about that."

"The kid was meant to get shot," Eddie told him. "Only he didn't. My team ended up running round like headless chickens, trying to catch him. So now Joe Hatton is bound to testify against the three of them. And there's a thing I forgot to mention earlier – they've got my bloke in the police. Soon they'll work out that I was the one who shot their inspector, if they haven't already."

"*You* did that? You're kidding! I heard you had an alibi…" Gordon looked shocked. He couldn't see Eddie as a killer.

That was the way Eddie wanted it. He explained.

"The guy who checked up on my alibi was Phil Church, the bent copper. I gave him a hundred grand to confirm that he'd seen me in Glasgow on the night in question. But I'd already gone back to Nottingham to save the others' skins. If the rest of the team had only agreed to retire a couple of weeks earlier, like I wanted, we'd all be home clear by now. There was no risk to me, so I let them talk me round. Big mistake."

His old friend listened intently, wide-eyed and gormless. Eddie finished his explanation.

"You see, Gordon, I'm the boss. I've always been the boss. Sooner or later, the police are bound to work that out. Not yet, maybe, but next week, next year, whenever … so I'm going to have to change ID, disappear completely."

"I see," Gordon said. "That's bad news."

"Yeah. Especially for you. See, if you hadn't staged that fake robbery in the first place, none of this would have happened."

"I don't know about that," Gordon said, beginning to shiver.

"I do. You're a liability, Gordon, but I'm going to do you a favour."

"What?" Gordon's eyes narrowed. Maybe there was still some kind of chance, he seemed to be thinking.

"I'm going to take that money in your case. Some of it I'm gonna use for the additional expenses you've caused me. My boys can't get at their own money for lawyers without it being traced. So they'll use yours. And, whatever's left, I'll make sure it gets to Maxine and Natalie. They'll think it comes from you, which is more than you deserve. They'll think you're still alive."

"Alive?" Suddenly, Gordon's eyes opened wide.

"But you're not."

Eddie shot him twice in the heart, at point-blank range, then kicked his body into the pit.

It was easier the second time, he reflected, killing someone. He got the spade out of the car and filled the grave quickly, for he was a healthy, well built man, unlike Gordon, who was a walking candidate for a heart attack. When Eddie was done, he got a move on, changing his suit for casual gear. The suit would contain gunpowder traces, together with earth and Gordon's blood, so he would dump it later. There was an incinerator he could visit after dark.

Eddie tucked the money into his own case. Would he use some of it to pay for the team's defence? Probably not. There was no honour among thieves – they'd agreed that all along, and kept their money separate. Let the others fend for themselves.

Eddie would tell Shirley that Gordon had never showed up. Maybe he'd bung Maxine and Natalie a little money, when it was safe. Let them think it came from Gordon. And he'd look after Julie, of course, and Tammy, and even Curt, as soon as he safely could. Shirley wanted him to fetch the kids over when they were settled. But once the police worked out what Eddie had done, they'd watch those three like hawks. It would never be safe for them to visit. No need to tell Shirley that, not yet anyway.

Oh well, Eddie thought, *it's over now*. He put some Vivaldi on the stereo and drove on into the lush countryside, stopping only to burn his soiled clothes and phone Shirley.

"I'll be home in a couple of hours, duck," he said, like any husband kept unexpectedly late at the office.

What happens next? Read

VICTIMS

and find out…

PROLOGUE

Imagine a situation. It's the quiet time of the afternoon. You go to the corner shop for a can, which is all you can afford. Walk in. The bell rings. No one's there.

"Just a minute," calls a voice from the back.

And you wait, surrounded by sweets, cigarettes, newspapers and magazines, all there for the taking. You know this shop. There's no hidden video camera. The newsagent's only just taken over. He's a bit green, or he wouldn't leave the place unattended, not round here. You're wearing a coat with big pockets: a shoplifter's special. All you have to do is reach out and…

The door rings again and you breathe a sigh of relief. Saved by the bell. The boy who enters is from your school. He's in your year, but you don't know each other.

"You doing a paper round here?" he asks. You shake your head.

"Where's the old man?"

"In the back."

"Nice one."

And the youth reaches over the counter, grabbing two packets of twenty. In a flash they're on your side of the counter and he's proffering one of them towards you.

"No, thanks," you say. "I don't smoke."

The youth shrugs and shoves both packets in his pocket before Mr Simons comes back through.

"You're early, Trevor," he says.

"No school. We've got an INSET day."

"Aah. Well, I've nearly finished making up the papers." He turns your way. "And what can I do for you, son?"

You buy your can and leave in a hurry. You've resisted temptation. Cigarettes are no longer the only thing that you've given up. Your girlfriend will be proud of you. Your sister will be proud of you. Your mother, on the other hand, would tell you off for not taking the fags and giving them to her. But Mum's opinion doesn't matter any more. This time, she's taken off for good.

You turn the corner for home and there's someone knocking on the door. Woman. Mid-thirties.

Dressed smartly but badly, the way certain middle-class women do when they don't want to be thought of as female. You don't like the look of this woman, but it's too late. She's seen you.

"Hi, I'm your new social worker. We need to have a little chat."

She holds out a hand like you're really going to shake it. Behind her, the door opens. Your sister's standing there and the woman is distracted, turns to introduce herself. It's decision time again. What do you do?

Because you know why this woman is here. She's come to take you into care. You know what care's like: a cacky children's home where half the girls are on the game and some of the lads, too. It's the last place on earth that you want to go.

So here's the choice: stay put and bluff it out, or do a runner. Your social worker is turning back towards you. The next eighteen months of your life hinge on the decision you're about to take.

Make up your mind.

1

Riverside Estates was an exclusive development on the city side of the river Trent, a short walk from the cricket, and both football, grounds. Most of these trendy, architect-designed places on the river were for singles or child-free couples, but Riverside was aimed at families. The apartments were low, streamlined buildings in reddish-brown brick, with big windows and double garages. Ben wouldn't mind living somewhere like that himself, maybe even with Julie, if he could afford it.

Funny, Ben had never hankered after living with a woman before, but Julie brought out the nesting instinct in him. He'd grown fond of Tammy. She ought to have a brother or sister to play with before the age gap grew too big. Not that he and Julie had discussed stuff like that. It was early days. If it weren't for the Inspector putting pressure on him to finish with her, Ben probably wouldn't be thinking this way. He didn't like people telling him what to do in his private life.

Gary, his partner, thought Ben was mad, going out with a Wilder. But Gary was gay and therefore, Ben reckoned, couldn't tell how good-looking Julie was. Nor did he know how nurturing, smart and sincere she was. He knew nothing.

"I think it's this one," Gary said now.

"Right you are."

They found the address from where someone had dialled 999. Gary didn't know that today was Ben's birthday, and Ben wanted to keep it that way. As expected, Ruth had said nothing in the Parade room that morning. From now on, Ben wanted to keep his private and his professional work totally separate. It wasn't as if any of the other officers were friends of his outside the job (ex-girlfriends didn't count, he decided). He and Neil were friends, but Neil was no longer in uniform.

"This is it."

Number 12A. Funny how some places still avoided using thirteen. You'd have thought that superstition was well on the way out, like years with a one on the front of them, but no. And the ersatz number had turned out to be unlucky all the same.

The mother came to the door. As Gary talked,

Ben sized her up. Jenny Jackson was a thirty-something professional who'd taken time out from Telecom management to have a kid, just the one, and went back to work within a couple of months. She shared a nanny with a neighbour in a similar situation, but the nanny was sick today and she'd had to take the day off work.

"Bridget, that's the woman I share the nanny with, was meant to be leaving work early to take over so that I could at least show my face at the office this afternoon. I'd left the door on the latch, so that she could walk in."

"As could anyone," Gary pointed out gently.

"Yes, but I was doing the laundry – it's hard to find the time – and I might not have heard the bell. Anyway, it's very safe round here."

Ben didn't comment. This development might attract people with a joint income well in excess of forty grand a year, but within five minutes (walking, not driving) you could find the highest percentage criminal population in the city, not to mention squats crawling with crackheads and hostels full of aging itinerant dossers who would probably prefer prison to their current life and, therefore, had nothing to stop them committing any criminal act which took their fancy.

"When did you last see Tom?" Gary asked.

"Three quarters of an hour ago. About one. He was playing in the living room, just round the corner from me. We were talking. He's picked up quite a few words. Then I took out one load, put in another, and when I looked again, he was gone."

"Does he walk yet?" Ben asked.

"Oh yes, he's two, so he walks quite a lot. Though he mainly crawls."

"Can he reach the doorknob?"

"Well, he tries. I've not seen him turn it yet, but, obviously, that was the first thing I thought. I've been round the neighbours, knocking on doors, finding out if anyone's seen him."

Wasted time, Ben knew, if the boy had been taken. She ought to have called the police straight away.

"All right," he said, taking over from Gary, who was only a probationer. "We'd better get a few more details. Do you have a recent photograph?"

When they were done, both men searched the apartment, which was standard procedure. Missing children sometimes turned out not to be missing, but hiding. They went from room to room, inspecting dust beneath beds, expensive clothes hung haphazardly in wardrobes, three TVs and two videos. But no kid. Ben radioed Inspector Winter.

"You'd better start a door-to-door. I'll inform CID, send John and Ruth over to help. You're on overtime."

Great. Overtime on his birthday. And working with Ruth. That was all Ben needed.

* * *

Half the apartments had no one home. The next shift would come around later when the owners were back from work. Not that they'd have seen anything. Ben met an assortment of nannies, housewives and harassed home workers. The owners were all of an age (mid-thirties) and a type (pretentious professional). One claimed to be an accountant.

"Look, I'm awfully busy. No, I haven't seen anything. Recognize him? No. Sorry. If I see anything I'll call you, but I've got a client coming round, so…" The man, who was short, and suffering from premature hair loss, began to close the door.

"I still need your name, sir, and the names of any other people living at this address."

"Here's my card. I live here alone."

The card said his name was Jeremy Tate. Peculiar that, Ben thought, as he joined Gary. Why would a single man be living in a three or four bedroom apartment? He made a note.

When they returned to 12A, Jenny Jackson was starting to crack up. Her son had been missing for nearly two hours. The enormity of the event was beginning to sink in. At least she'd been joined by her husband, Tony, who was comforting her. He was a good deal older than Jenny – mid-forties, maybe. Second marriage, Ben guessed. Second family.

"No news, I'm afraid."

Tony Jackson ignored Ben and turned to a figure

in an armchair. Ben hadn't noticed there was anybody else there.

"What do you do now?" he asked.

Neil Foster stood up, nodded at Ben, then went through the procedure in detail. This was CID's case now. Everyone deferred to the man who wasn't wearing a uniform. In the months since he'd moved to CID, Neil had changed. He dressed better. His haircut was neater, more stylish. Maybe it was the job. Or maybe it was the influence of his student girlfriend, Melanie.

"How's it going?" Neil asked as they walked out afterwards.

"Can't complain."

"There's a story going round that you're having it off with the Wilder girl – what's her name? – Julie."

"Who told you?" Ben asked, awkwardly.

"Jan mentioned it in passing," Neil said with a grin.

Neil remained friendly with Jan Hunt, who used to be his mentor. Was it her who'd told Winter? She wasn't a gossip, but might have regarded it as her responsibility.

"Not serious, is it?" Neil asked, catching Ben's uneasy mood.

"Serious enough."

"Happy birthday, anyway. Got plans?"

"Family stuff."

"Have a good one."

Actually, Ben was joining Julie as soon as he got off. They would spend the rest of the afternoon in bed, then she'd found a sitter for the evening, so they could go out for a meal."

"Hey, Neil!" said a familiar voice. Ruth Clarke.

"Hi, how are you?" Neil said, as Ben beat a hasty retreat from his ex. What was it with women and him, Ben wondered? One ex-girlfriend had followed him from London to Nottingham, where she worked as a criminal lawyer (Charlene's name had come up representing the pervert who got let out yesterday). He kept coming across her. Then his next ex went one better and actually moved on to the same shift as him less than a month after he'd dumped her! Mad. Totally mad.

As Ben closed the door, Ruth gave him one of *those* looks – a mixture of pain and contempt. He could have done without that on his birthday.

Charlene had been unable to palm off the interview on anyone else, so, at four on the afternoon after Alan Wallace had been freed, she met him to discuss his options.

"I lost nearly six months of my life," Wallace said.

"Yes, I know."

Charlene had prepared all the paperwork for the case. She'd advised Wallace that his "not guilty" plea had a good chance of success, while being privately convinced that he'd done exactly what was alleged, and a lot more.

"I had a job before I was arrested."

Not much of a job, actually, supervizing pork-pie packers at Pork Farms on 20p an hour over the old minimum rate. Before he had been convicted the first time, however, Wallace had been a deputy head at a Derbyshire Primary School.

"So what can I do?"

"You don't have many options, I'm afraid," Charlene said. "You see, from a legal point of view, the courts were entitled to keep you in custody while waiting for trial. The prosecution convinced the magistrates that there was a real risk of you either reoffending or interfering with the witnesses, who were vulnerable children."

"But none of them were willing to testify against me!" Wallace complained.

"True," Charlene said, "and if they were adults, you'd be entitled to pursue a compensation claim against them in a civil court, arguing that they made the story up to get at you. But they're kids – even if you were allowed to sue them, they haven't got any money."

"There must be some way I can claim," Wallace protested. "Isn't there some kind of Criminal Compensation Board?"

"That's for victims," Charlene explained, patiently, "not offenders."

"I am a victim," Wallace said, straightfaced.

Charlene clenched her fists beneath the desk. Sometimes, the human race's capacity for hypocrisy could still surprise her.

"Look," she said, "your only avenue of redress would be to sue the police for malicious prosecution."

"Let's do that then."

"However, I have to advise you that your chances of success are zero. The police acted properly all the way down the line. If you took them to court, all you'd be doing is drawing attention to yourself. Believe me, the media would have a field day."

"So you're saying that there's absolutely no way I can get any compensation?"

"That's right," Charlene said. "But look at it this way. You're free. You'll get benefit. It's much better than being in prison."

"Oh, thanks a lot," Wallace said, getting up. "My life's ruined and I'm supposed to be grateful that things aren't worse? Thanks a million!"

You were grateful enough yesterday when they dropped the charges, Charlene thought, but didn't say. She watched him go out, grateful herself, and said a silent prayer that their paths would never cross again.

Ben was asleep when the doorbell rang. At first he thought that he was at home, but then it rang again and he remembered that he was on the Maynard Estate. He'd done an hour and a half's overtime before being relieved and heading straight over to Julie's. Now it was five to five. The bell rang again. Tammy started to cry and Julie swore.

"I was going to pretend not to be in. Better answer it now."

She opened the window, yelled "Hold on!", then tidied herself up and went to the door. When Ben went after her, he watched from the stairs. There were two officers from the shift that replaced his in the front room: Mike Singh and Stuart Crane. With them was a woman who could only be Curt's social worker. The woman was talking.

"I'm sorry, Julie, but I checked your story with the holiday firm whose name you gave me. They haven't got a Shirley Wilder on their client list."

"I must have got it wrong."

"She's been gone nearly a month, Julie. I don't think she's coming back."

"So? Listen. If Mum doesn't come back, I can look after Curt. He's fifteen. I don't see what the problem is."

The social worker wasn't having that. "Curt isn't your problem, he's ours. You have a baby of your own to look after. I'm sure if you explain the situation, the council won't throw you out of this house. Housing Benefit will pay the rent. But you can't afford to support Curt."

"I manage."

"And it's not legal."

Ben worried. Was Julie cheating the DSS, like her mother used to? She'd promised Ben that she didn't break the law. But her concept of legality was flexible.

"I'm sorry, Julie," the social worker went on, "but you're still only a kid yourself."

That wasn't the way to talk to Julie.

"Just shut your mouth!" Julie shouted, sounding like her mother. "What right have you got to come in here, laying down the law? And why've you brought these bully boys with you, huh?"

It was a while since Ben had seen Julie's temper. He either had to make himself scarce or weigh in immediately. Happy birthday.

"We're here to help collect Curt," Mike Singh said, taking over. "Take him to the children's home. Where is he?"

"I don't know."

"You won't mind if we take a look…"

"Yes, I bloody do mind—"

"Hold on," Ben said, making himself known. The three invaders turned to face him. "Curt's not here. He's not coming back tonight, either."

"Where is he?" the social worker asked.

"I don't know," Ben said. "Look, can't we work this out?"

"He's in the job," one of the officers told the social worker.

"We can talk," the woman said. "But it won't make any difference…"